The Quest for Justice

By

Bill Shuey

Ulmer,
Best wishes
Bill Shuey
10/2021

1

Retribution
The Quest for Justice

Noun: punishment inflicted on someone as vengeance for a wrong or criminal act.

Other books by Bill Shuey

A Search for Israel

A Search for Bible Truth

Unholy Dilemma – A Search for Logic in
the Old Testament

Unholy Dilemma 2 – A Search for Logic in
the New Testament

Unholy Dilemma 3 – A Search for Logic in
the Qur'an

Have a good week – Ten years of
ObverseView musings

East of Edin

Retribution
The Quest for Justice

Retribution
The Quest for Justice

Revised – September 2020

ISBN 13: 978-1986245975
ISBN 10: 1986245977

Printed in the United States of America

This work is dedicated to my dad, Claude E. Shuey, who loved western novels, owned the entire Zane Gray library, and instilled in me the love of western yarns.

Acknowledgements

Many thanks to my sister-in-law Bernice (Bern) who proof-reads my books and articles without compensation and lends me her time without complaint. Since I struggled with high school English and she taught young ladies in the college environment, her assistance is vital.

And to Doris Jo Lewis the newest member of the team, whose English skills put a needed polish on my work.

And Marisa Mott – www.cowboykimono.com for the cover wrap.

And last but never least, to my wife, Gloria, who has encouraged me for years to write books of fiction and suffers my hours on a word processor without complaint.

Chapter 1

Homer Barthelme "Bart" Strong had the ideal life: a comfortable home in Bolivar, Missouri, and a wonderful family. His only child was a beautiful daughter who would soon become a teenager and was the apple of his eye. He was lucky to have a wife who doted on him, and he catered to her. They were the perfect family. Then, the Confederate States Army decided to bombard Fort Sumter on April 12, 1861 and turned Bart's life upside down.

Prior to the beginning of the Civil War, Bart was a deputy sheriff for Polk County, Missouri. While on duty with the sheriff's department, Bart carried a Colt 1855 Sidehammer, also known as the Colt Root revolver, in .31 caliber. Even though he carried the sidearm, people who had seen him shoot the pistol went away laughing. He couldn't hit the broadside of a barn with the revolver. Bart took the good-natured ribbing in stride, probably because he knew it was true. What Bart lacked in pistol skill, he more than made up for in his use of his Whitworth .451 caliber rifle he had purchased for more than he could afford at the time. With the Whitworth, there were few men who were his equal as a marksman.

****

The Whitworth Rifle was a single-shot muzzle-loaded rifle used in the latter half of the 19th century. The Whitworth was an excellent long-range weapon for its time and was, with the addition of a scope, the world's first sniper rifle. The Whitworth was used by Confederate sharpshooters in the Civil War and, in the hands of a competent sharpshooter, could hit targets up to 1,000 yards away. The rifle was responsible for claiming the lives of several Union generals including John F. Reynolds, the highest-ranking Union officer killed at Gettysburg. The Whitworth was considered to be the very best rifle of the period in terms of accuracy.

Confederate soldiers that used the Whitworth rifles were referred to as Whitworth Sharpshooters, and their main function was to eliminate Union artillery gun crews. But the sharpshooters were also used to harass Union officers.

On May 9, 1864, during the Battle of Spotsylvania Courthouse, Union General John Sedgwick was chiding his troops for lying in a ditch to avoid the gunfire from Confederate sharpshooters who were shooting from some 800 to 1,000 yards away. The whistling noise the Whitworth's hexagonal bullets made in flight would make members of his staff and artillerymen duck for cover. Sedgwick told his men that he was ashamed of them for being scared and dodging for cover and said that the Confederate shooters couldn't hit an elephant from the distance they were shooting. Seconds later, a bullet struck Sedgwick just below his left eye. At least five Confederate soldiers claimed to have fired the fatal round. Bart wasn't one of the five. His goal was to only wound his targets. The goal of only wounding men was to change later in his life.

****

Unfortunately, in the here and now shooting at someone on a Union artillery crew or an officer was the least of Bart's problems. Normally, one of the officers that lead the scouts would inform him of where the Union patrols were located, then he could skirt shy of them and make it to the location he was headed. Getting back to the Rebel lines was the problem.

On April 8th, 1862, Bart and the rest of Colonel Nathan Buford Forrest's troops were camped near the Confederate field hospital, tasked with the responsibility of protecting the injured men and Surgeon William D. Lyles. The location was called

Fallen Timbers because of the large number of dead trees in the area.

Union Brigadier General William T. Sherman's scouts found the lightly protected hospital and advanced towards it.

Bart was returning from a reconnaissance mission and found himself in the middle of a skirmish. Colonel Forrest charged the advancing Union infantry brigade alone, not by choice, but because, unbeknownst to Forrest, his cavalry had stopped their charge.

Colonel Forrest found himself completely surrounded. He started firing his Colt Army revolvers and fired at the soldiers until he ran out of ammunition, pulled his saber and began hacking and slashing at the Union soldiers.

Bart was well hidden and had a choice to make; fire to help the colonel and give up his position or stay in hiding. Bart selected a Union captain who seemed to be in charge and fired. The impact of the bullet spun the Union officer around and he fell face-first to the ground. Bart reloaded as quickly as he could, picked another target that was close to Colonel Forrest and fired again. Reloaded and fired again.

The Union infantry were in disarray and withdrawing. A Union soldier who was just a few feet from Colonel Forrest fired his rifle musket and the ball went through the Confederate colonel's pelvis and lodged near his spine.

Bart ran to the colonel, slung the Whitworth over his shoulder, and helped hold him in the saddle, and started walking towards the Confederate lines.

Before they had progressed more than a few yards, Bart felt a sting in his left arm and then another bullet that jarred him.

A cavalry captain and two troopers rode out to Colonel Forrest and Bart and took them to the field hospital. The bullet which had hit Bart's arm went all the way through, and other than producing a good bit of bleeding, wasn't serious.

The bullet that had hit him in the back was another matter. Bart and Colonel Forrest lay in the field hospital until the area was secured and the delicate surgery on both men could be attempted.

Doctor Lyles removed the bullet from Colonel Forrest. Forrest thanked the surgeon and said, "Treat that corporal, he probably saved my life." The surgeon dug around in Bart's chest and finally got ahold of the bullet with retractors and pulled it out.

There was no anesthesia available, so Bart and Colonel Forrest were forced to endure their surgeries while biting on pieces of boot leather.

Colonel Forrest was back on his horse the day following surgery. Bart stayed in the ward one extra day and then rejoined the regiment.

Chapter 2

On the early morning of July 10, 1862, Corporal Bart Strong left the Confederate camp to look for targets of opportunity, specifically officers, around Murfreesboro, Tennessee. On the afternoon of the 11th, Bart had gone thirty-six hours without rest or sleep and was give out. He led his chestnut colored Morgan into a dry creek bed, pulled the horse down, and lay beside the animal.

A sound woke Bart up and he sat up with a start to see a Union sergeant smiling at him and four other soldiers with rifles pointed at him. "Well, Johnny Reb, it looks like you picked a poor time and place to take a nap," and hit Bart in the gonads with the butt of his rifle musket.

"Stand up, Corporal. Oh, I'm sorry, I guess you need a couple minutes to get your privates back in order." Bart took a few deep breaths, the pain began to subside somewhat, and he tried to get up. As he was struggling to his feet, the sergeant grabbed Bart by his blouse with his left hand and hit him in the mouth with his right fist.

While Bart was spitting blood, the sergeant said, "We don't much cotton to Rebel sharpshooters. I expect you'll face a firing squad tomorrow. Maybe they'll let us be the ones to shoot you. The sergeant got tickled and said to no one in particular, "Don't cotton, that's a good one."

Corporal Melvin Jones and Private Jimmy Johns were hiding in a clump of trees as the Union detail walked by and saw they had Corporal Strong as their prisoner. They didn't know how many other patrols were in the area, so they headed back to the Confederate camp.

Corporal Jones scurried off, found Captain William "Bill" Brubaker and told him what they had seen with regard to Corporal Strong. Captain Brubaker walked to the headquarters tent and told Colonel Forrest what the scouts had reported with regard to Strong.

"Well, Captain, I probably have Corporal Strong to thank for my life, I guess it's as good a time as any to return the favor. Go to Murfreesboro under a flag of truce and see if you can arrange a prisoner swap."

Captain Brubaker saluted and said, "Yes, Sir." Captain Brubaker got his mount, a large piece of white linen, and started for the Union lines outside of Murfreesboro. When he neared the encampment, he tied the cloth on his saber and held it up so that the Union soldiers would see the emblem of truce and not shoot him.

When he rode into the camp, a captain walked up and said, "Reb, you've got a lot of hard bark on you riding into a Union camp all by yourself. Maybe more bark than brains. What do you want?"

"Captain, you have a prisoner that Colonel Nathan Forrest would like to have released. He is willing to swap one of your captains and a lieutenant for Corporal Strong."

"Captain Reb, your corporal is a sharpshooter, he is going to be shot by a firing squad tomorrow morning."

"Captain, I have it to understand that Brigadier General Crittenden is the commander of this unit, you would do well to get him, and let me talk to the general. I think he will be interested in the two prisoners we want to swap."

The Union captain was thoughtful for a few moments and decided that he would err on the side of caution and had a sergeant go to find General Crittenden.

When General Crittenden walked up, he said, "What's so important that it requires my presence, Captain?"

"Sir, begging the general's pardon, but this Reb captain says that you would want to know the prisoners that Colonel Forrest wants to exchange."

General Crittenden looked at Captain Brubaker and said, "OK. Let's hear your story, Captain."

"Sir, we have two Union officers. A Captain Michael Smallwood and a shave-tail lieutenant named Marshal Sherman. I've been asked by Colonel Forrest to advise you that if Corporal Strong's execution isn't stopped and he isn't released forthwith, Captain Smallwood will be executed after you kill Strong."

Captain Brubaker gave the general a few moments to digest what he had said, and continued, "As to Lieutenant Sherman, he will be sent to the Confederate prison in Vicksburg, Mississippi, to spend the remainder of this war. That presumes that he lives until the end of the war, which isn't a given in prison camp. Colonel Forrest hopes that you will see the wisdom of sparing General Sherman's nephew the horrible ordeal of the prison."

"Captain, how do I know that you have this Lieutenant Sherman in captivity?"

"General, you have my word of honor that we have Lieutenant Sherman in chains at our camp."

General Crittenden was thoughtful for a few moments, turned to the Union captain, and said, "Arrange the prisoner swap with the Rebel captain. I want to see

17

Lieutenant Sherman when the prisoner swap is concluded."

At 3 PM, on the 12th of July, Captain Brubaker and two Rebel cavalry troopers led Captain Smallwood and Lieutenant Sherman to a small clearing between the Union and Confederate camps. Captain Brubaker had the troopers remove the manacles off the two Union officers and told them to walk to the captain and his detail. Corporal Strong walked to Captain Brubaker leading the chestnut and with the Whitworth over his shoulder.

When the Union captain got Captain Smallwood and Lieutenant Sherman to the Union camp, he took the lieutenant to see General Crittenden straightaway.

Lieutenant Sherman had no idea why a general would want to see him but tagged along. When they arrived at the general's tent, the captain announced him, and the general asked the lieutenant to come inside. The lieutenant saluted and General Crittenden told him to stand easy. "Lieutenant, I hope you will tell General Sherman that I secured your release from the Rebels."

"Well, General, if I ever see him, I'll be sure to tell him."

"Lieutenant, if you will get a letter to your family, I'm sure they will notify the general that his nephew is safe."

"Sir, with all due respect, my uncle is a farmer in Ohio. As far as I know, we're not related to General Sherman."

General Crittenden burst out laughing and said, "Well, I've been hornswoggled, no doubt about that. That Rebel captain sure put one over on me. He didn't come right out and say that you were General Sherman's nephew, but he sure left that implication. Pretty slick."

When they got back to the Confederate camp, Captain Brubaker said, "I don't think Colonel Forrest will go out of his way to save your bacon again. I wouldn't get caught again if I were you."

On the 13th, Colonel Forrest's cavalry force attacked the Union forces protecting Murfreesboro.

The Union garrison surrendered to Colonel Forrest. Forrest had his men destroy Union supplies and much of the railroad tracks close to the town. The main success of the engagement was that it slowed the Union Army's advance towards Chattanooga.

On July 21, 1862, Colonel Nathan Buford Forrest was promoted to brigadier general.

On the same day, a certain Union sergeant was in the infirmary recovering from a gunshot wound to his right hand. The .451 bullet from a Whitworth had pretty much shattered the man's hand. The abusive sergeant was alive, but if he wanted to hit another defenseless man in the mouth, he would have to use his left fist to strike the blow.

Chapter 3

The year was 1879. The Civil War had been over for the better part of thirteen years, but the deep-seated animosity regarding the destruction of the South during the war and the harsh treatment the former rebels received during the Reconstruction Period lingered on. Work was scarce, and money even scarcer. Some good men turned bad, and some bad men got worse, much worse. The seven men who rode into Hall County, Texas, on the September morning were a mixture of former Confederate soldiers, carpetbaggers, scalawags, hired killers, bank robbers, and arsonists, and one mixed breed who murdered just for fun.

Cherokee Joe was neither Cherokee nor named Joe. He was half Arapaho and half Negro. As a young boy, he had been called *kooxo'ooteihinoo wo'oo*, "I am Slow Foot," by the people in the Arapaho village in which he grew up, but the white settlers called him Arapanigger. Or at least they did until he killed one of them outside a dry goods store in Tucson, Arizona, when he was fourteen. Slow Foot always dreamed of being a Cherokee warrior and started calling himself Cherokee Joe. Joe after a Missouri farmer named Joe Blakefield he had killed with a knife. After the killing of the settler, friends and foes alike called him Cherokee Joe. Joe had dark skin, dark hair, dark eyes, and a dark soul. He was riding a dun gelding with a mixture of yellow and brown on its body and dark legs. Joe was armed with an 1860 Spencer repeater rifle and an 1860 Colt Army model revolver carried in a waist wrap. He also carried his weapon of choice which was a razor-sharp single edge blade made by a blacksmith who copied James Bowie's "Iron Mistress." Joe was hatless and wore his hair long in side braids. Joe was neither big nor little, just average in size, but what he lacked in size he more than made up for in brutality.

Buryl Weathers was the oldest and leader of the gang of misfits. Weathers had been a scout for the Gray during the Civil War and had managed to avoid detection and capture for more than three years, no small task with Union patrols searching for him almost constantly. Weathers preferred a knife over a gun because stealth was his only method of survival during the war years. He carried two Sheffield Bowie knives in Government Issue sheaths and could throw them with amazing accuracy. He also carried one of the new Colt Peacemakers he had taken off a man he had robbed and killed. Buryl was a large man with curly black hair, graying at the temples, a long straight nose, piercing gray eyes, a strong chin, and a gunfighter type moustache which was stained with tobacco juice. His appearance alone would deter the hardiest of men.

Slade Johnson was the youngest of the bunch, barely eighteen, but already having the dubious distinction of having killed two men. One was a Negro, the other an Indian, and neither was in fair fights. Johnson was a sneaky little bastard, and bastard was the correct word because his mother was a prostitute in Oklahoma City, Oklahoma, and had absolutely no idea of the identity of Slade's father. In fact, the first man Slade killed was a Negro who called him "son" as he was leaving Slade's mother's brothel room after sampling her wares. The second was an Indian who called him a bastard. Slade was a little sensitive regarding his lineage. Johnson was barely 5' 7" tall in his boots, fair of skin and hair, and displayed little in the way of facial whiskers. He carried an 1858 Remington Navy .36 caliber pistol he had taken off the Indian he killed, and a Model 1851 .54 caliber Sharps rifle he had stolen from an unconscious drunk. The 1851 model was the first mass produced Sharps by Robbins & Lawrence Company of Windsor, Vermont.

Bevis Smith was a drunk and deserter from the Confederate Army. Smith joined the Gray army in 1863 while he was living with his parents in Jasper County, Missouri. He was a lay-about who couldn't hold a job, and when his father got tired of feeding him, he told him to join the army or find someplace else to live. He chose the army. On April 8, 1864, Smith received a minor wound in a skirmish in Mansfield, Louisiana, deserted the next day, and drifted back to Jasper County. He managed to hide out with some other lowlifes and then went to Texas after the war. Smith worked on a few cattle drives but wasn't much of a hand and was never rehired. He committed a couple petty thefts, stabbed a city marshal during his last arrest, and spent three years in the Texas State prison at Huntsville, Texas, north of Houston. While serving his three-year stint in Huntsville, Smith met Buryl Weathers in 1877, and so began their association. Smith was about 6' 0" tall, heavy framed, redheaded and wore a long red beard. He wasn't much of a shot with a handgun and only carried an 1853 Slant-Breech Sharps .54 caliber carbine.

Charles Daile was a former carpetbagger who had avoided the war and then come south from New York to profiteer during the Reconstruction Era. Daile was caught price gouging and shot an Austin, Texas, town deputy while resisting arrest. The deputy lived, but Daile was found guilty of attempted murder in June of 1867 and sentenced to 10 years at hard labor in the state prison at Huntsville, Texas. During his stay at Huntsville, Daile met Buryl Weathers. Daile was a coward, and if he was going to fight at all, it would be from behind and by surprise. He had only killed one man, having shot him in the back in San Saba, Texas. After losing a hand in a poker game that wiped him out, Daile hid in an alley, waited for the winner to come down the dark sidewalk, and shot him as he walked past. Daile was slight of frame, had thinning hair, a sparsely bearded pockmarked face, a weak chin, shifty blue eyes, and always avoided holding eye contact. He carried an old .36 caliber Colt Paterson revolver with a 12" barrel and an American Arms double barrel 12-gauge shotgun.

William Jay (Wil) Gabbage was a scalawag who collaborated with the Northern carpetbaggers during reconstruction. He got caught trying to sell a load of grain which didn't belong to him and was tarred and feathered and ran out of Sulphur Springs, Texas. Gabbage drifted from one frontier town to another, rolling drunks and working the occasional odd job. In April 1874, Gabbage and two other no-accounts he had met decided to rob the dry goods store in Brashear, Texas. The town marshal and a couple good citizens were waiting for Gabbage and his associates when they came out of the store. The two associates were killed, and Gabbage received a bullet to the leg which left him with a permanent limp and a free ride to Huntsville prison where he met Weathers, Smith, and Daile. Gabbage was heavy set with curly brown hair and beard and carried a pistol and rifle. He had never killed anyone but only because he wasn't a very good shot and always got nervous and fidgety when under pressure.

Last, but not least, in this rogues cast was James Madison Smart, a hired killer of some reputation and known for his ruthlessness and disregard for human life. Smart was a good-looking guy. Based on appearance, one would think him more suited for the theatre than the life of a killer. Tall and rangy, Smart was always clean shaven with well-groomed light brown hair and steely green eyes. Smart had little sense of humor and had killed men, thirteen so far, most for supposed minor infractions against his honor. Smart carried two of the new Colt Peacemakers in cross-draw fashion, one on each hip.

Such was the group which slowly rode in single file through the rolling hills of Hall County, Texas, looking for cattle, horses, or money to steal.

Chapter 4

Nettie Lea Strong came into this world on April 1, 1851, the first and only child of Homer Barthelme (Bart) and Mary Elizabeth Strong. Nettie was a strong-willed child, precocious but never belligerent or disobedient. She approached her studies with interest and determination and helped her mother around the house and with the outdoor chores.

Nettie's dad left to go to fight in the Civil War when she was almost thirteen years old. She could remember him, but his face had become fainter as time went on. Nettie and her mother managed to survive the long conflict and keep the home in Bolivar, Missouri, in good repair. Her mother was very lonely, but Nettie had lots of friends and spent considerable time helping her mother with household chores.

The horrible war ended on May 13, 1865, and her dad arrived back home the middle of June of that same year. Her dad wouldn't talk about the war or his function during the conflict. All he would say was the war was over, and it was time to get on to better things.

Nettie's dad was well respected and fairly old at forty-seven when he left to serve the south in the war. Most men nearing fifty years of age found some reason to avoid the war. Bart Strong wanted to do his duty and defend his home and property from what he saw as an invasion by the Union. Bart was a man of strong conviction who felt joining the conflict was his obligation.

When Strong came home from the war, Governor Thomas C. Fletcher appointed him as sheriff of Polk County, Missouri. Since the county seat was in Bolivar, the Strong family remained in their home.

Bart quickly realized that he was just swapping one conflict for another. Missouri was a hotbed of violence.

****

After four years of bitter conflict, Missourians were looking forward to a peaceful future. On January 11, 1865, the Missouri state convention passed an emancipation ordinance which immediately freed all slaves in Missouri.

Charles D. Drake was a member of the Radical Party which spearheaded the emancipation ordinance. At Drake's insistence, the Missouri state constitution was altered to include an "iron-clad oath" which required that individuals disavow having been involved in eighty-six acts of disloyalty against Missouri and the Union.

The acts ranged from providing money, goods, or intelligence to the Confederacy to actually having taken up arms against the Union. Even expressing sympathy for the South would be viewed as an act of disloyalty. Failing to take the oath would prevent one from voting, holding a public office, or from holding a professional license such as lawyers, teachers, and even the clergy.

Both Missouri and Arkansas saw the emergence of guerrilla violence in the post-war years. Jesse James became the face of post-war violence. He and his gang of Quantrill leftovers robbed banks and killed citizens in broad daylight.

****

Bart couldn't sign the oath because he had served in the Confederate Army, but Governor Fletcher's appointment overrode any need for an oath.

On February 13, 1866, a group of outlaws robbed the Polk County Saving Association in Bolivar, Missouri, killed a young man who was merely walking down the street, and made off with $60,000.00 in greenbacks.

When Sheriff Strong got to the savings association and walked inside, he saw the clerk on the floor with a gash in his skull. He was breathing, but the breaths were shallow, and he was bleeding badly.

When Bart questioned the bystanders, he found that there were six men involved in the robbery; three that went inside, one was stationed outside the bank door, and two stayed with the horses. He got a general description of the men, the type of horses they were riding, and even a couple distinguishing features of the bandits. No one seemed to know if it was the James gang, but it would be coincidental if it was anything but.

Bart went home, told Mary and Nettie what had happened and that he was going to get a posse together and go after the robbers. After informing them, he took his Whitworth off the wall and picked up his shotgun. He headed for the Bolivar Saloon to see if he could round up any volunteers to accompany him.

When he entered the bat-wing doors, Bart saw the normal crowd. It was mostly men shooting the bull and having a beer or two. Bart walked up to the bar, turned around, and said loud enough for everyone in the room to hear, "I'm going after the six men who robbed the savings association and could sure use some help if any of you are willing to act as deputies."

Six men put down their beers and said that they would go with the sheriff. Bart told the men to get their horses and meet him at the sheriff's office.

When Bart got his horse saddled and walked him to the sheriff's office there were six men of differing vocations standing by their horses.

Two were out of work former Union soldiers, one a farmer, one a gambler, and three businessmen in Bolivar. Bart swore in all six men and they mounted their horses and headed out of town. Bart stopped at a run-down shack on the edge of town and talked to an Osage Indian named Two Feathers who agreed to track the robbers for the posse.

The bandits had headed west on one of the main roads out of Bolivar towards Stockton. Stockton was in Cedar County, but Bart didn't think that would make much difference if the men went there.

Two Feathers rode along on his mule and watched to see if and when the bandits left the main road. About ten miles out of Bolivar, the tracks of six horses left the main road and headed across a field of prairie grass. Bart seemed to remember a farm being in the direction the men were taking, but wasn't certain his memory was accurate.

About a mile later, they were looking at a farmhouse and a large barn in the distance. Two Feathers followed the tracks, stopped about 200 yards from the farmhouse, and said, "They go there."

Bart told the posse members to fan out around the barn and wait for his signal before firing their weapons. He watched as the men took their positions around the barn and then rode up to the farmhouse. When Sheriff Strong got to the porch, a man walked out and said, "What can I do for you, Sheriff?"

Bart watched the man's body language and could tell that he was nervous; mighty nervous. "Six men robbed the savings association in Bolivar and killed at least one man. My tracker followed their horses' tracks to your farm. Have you seen them?"

"I don't know anything about any six men. There's no one here but me and my wife and kids."

"What is your name, Mister?"

"Jackson Brand. This is my farm and it's all I've got, Sheriff."

"You don't have to say anything, Mr. Brand, just nod your head. Are the bandits in your barn?"

"Sheriff, if I do anything to help you, they'll burn me out."

Bart turned his horse towards the barn and rode over beside the double doors and hollered, "There's seven men that have this barn surrounded, come out and we'll go back to Bolivar and you can stand trial."

There was no response and in a few moments six men came out of the barn with their horses at a gallop. Bart got off two shots with the shotgun and two men were knocked out of their saddles by the impact of the loads of buckshot.

The posse members managed to hit one of the bandits, but they got away. One of the former Union soldiers was shot by the bandits and was on the ground dead, and the gambler was toting a hunk of lead.

Four of the bandits had ridden off and Sheriff Strong had two dead bandits, one dead posse member, and one wounded man to deal with. He decided to take the bodies back to Bolivar, get some provisions, and start out again.

Chapter 5

The former Union soldier had no known kin in Polk County and no one would admit knowing the two dead bandits. Bart deposited the three bodies with the town undertaker and asked the four remaining uninjured posse members if they wanted to get back with him to try to find and arrest the four bandits; none did. The sight of dead men seemed to take the starch out of the posse members, and they didn't want to be the next ones killed.

Bart went home to get a bite to eat before heading out again. It was getting late in the afternoon and he wanted to get back to the barn so that Two Feathers could start tracking the four remaining bandits. "Bart, let them go. You killed two of them. Four men who are good with weapons are more than you need to take on by yourself."

"Mary, this isn't something I want to do. It is my job and something I have to do. If we can't find them in a couple days, I'll give up the chase and come back home."

Sheriff Strong and Two Feathers rode out of Bolivar headed for the Brand farm. When they got reasonably close, the smell of smoke was in the air, when they got closer, they saw the smoldering barn. The bandits had obviously returned and burned Brand's barn in retaliation for what they thought was his betrayal of them. When Bart looked at the small corral, both plow horses had been shot and were lying on the ground.

Brand, his wife, and two daughters were sitting on the porch. "I told you that they would burn me out. I don't have the money to rebuild the barn and all the hay went up in the flames. They didn't kill the milk cows, but now I have nothing to feed them this winter."

"I'm sorry for your loss, I truly am, but once they rode on your property they put you in a bad position. Do you know any of the men. Is there anything you can tell me that will help me to identify them?"

"I can tell you that none of them were Jesse or Frank James. I know them. These men were part of the killers from Quantrill's group, but I don't know their names. One of them is in a bad way. He has a bullet in his chest. One has blonde hair and walks with a limp. The other two are just average looking men."

Bart thanked Mr. Brand and asked if he could sleep on his porch. After getting permission, he and Two Feathers took the saddles off their mounts, put them down on the porch, picketed the horses where they could nibble on grass, and stretched out for the night.

The next morning, Bart was up early, accepted a cup of coffee from Mr. Brand, saddled his horse and he and Two Feathers got started following the tracks of the four men's horses.

The four men were traveling slowly, no doubt because of the wounded man. As the day progressed, it became obvious that the men were headed for Stockton. There really wasn't much else in the direction they were traveling.

The tracks led through three or four farms, but the men never got close to a farm house. Around three miles from Stockton, Bart came to a rise overlooking the Sac River. There were four men camped at the side of the river next to a copse of trees. Bart pulled his field glasses out of his haversack and took a look.

There was a man leaning up against a tree who had blood all over the front of his shirt and wasn't moving. Another man had blonde hair and the other two, as Mr. Brand had said, just looked average.

After confirming that he had the right four men, Bart dismounted, pulled his Whitworth out of its scabbard, spread his ground cover, and took a prone position. He debated for a few moments on what he wanted to do. They had killed a young man for no reason other than meanness and burned down Mr. Brand's barn and killed his work horses; he owed them no consideration. Still he hated to kill a man. He took aim at the blonde haired man, engaged the set trigger, and slowly squeezed. The big rifle belched fire and black smoke.

The shot was around 400 yards and comparatively easy. The bullet hit the man in the thigh and tore a large hole in his leg. The other two men were trying to get the saddles on their horses while Bart was reloading. He engaged the set trigger and slowly squeezed again. The man nearest him went down in a heap and didn't move. The last man who was mobile got on his horse and started across the river.

The land across the river was flat and nothing present that would impede seeing the man ride away. The man was more than 500 yards away and increasing the distance. Bart engaged the set trigger one last time, slowly squeezed and the big rifle belched fire and black smoke. A second or so later the man tumbled off his horse.

Bart got up, found some twigs, and got a small fire started and then added a few pieces of wood. He got his coffee cup out of his haversack and brewed a cup of coffee.

Two Feathers just sat and watched. He had done his job.

After waiting thirty minutes or so, Bart put the Whitworth back in the scabbard, mounted, and started down the hill. "Come with me Two Feathers, you can help me load the bodies on their horses."

"I go across river and get the other man, Sheriff."

When Bart rode into the bandits camp, the man leaning against the tree was dead, the man Bart had shot while he was mounting his horse was dead, and the blonde was in no condition to put up any kind of fight.

Bart got off his horse and walked to the blonde. He was bleeding and had a large hole in his leg, but he would live to hang. In about twenty minutes Two Feathers rode across the river with a man draped across his saddle.

Sheriff Strong rode into Bolivar with three dead men, one wounded man, and a sack of money from the savings association. Four days later, the blonde, Marcus Weatherford was hanged in the town square.

Chapter 6

Bart Strong served out the partial term, and was elected by the people of Polk County to a full term. He served part of the full term while taking law courses and then was elected county judge. Judge Strong was known as an honest and fair arbiter of the law. Unless the defendant had harmed a woman or child, there was a good chance he would find leniency. But if he had harmed a woman or child, he had better come to court prepared for a long stay in jail or state prison.

During the winter of 1867, Mary Elizabeth Strong fell ill and died within a couple of weeks due to complications of pneumonia. While the loss was devastating to Nettie, the loss of her mother threw her father into a period of depression. It didn't seem anything could console her father no matter what she tried: his favorite apple pie or fried pork chops or biscuits with red-eye gravy; nor did anything else seem to be of any interest to him. He drank too much for a time and would become sullen and insolent when Nettie pleaded with him to stop the drinking.

Finally, Nettie got up one morning, and her dad was sitting at the kitchen table drinking a cup of coffee, smiling, and appearing like his old self. He acted like the previous few weeks had never happened! He had gone through a long black tunnel, conquered his grief and demons, and came out the other side. Nettie was bewildered but very happy to have her father back. Judge Strong was on the bench and seemed happy to be working.

In the spring of 1869, Nettie was at Baker's dry goods store purchasing some flour, salt, sugar, and other necessities when in walked Jeffrey Blake Spencer, and her whole world changed and got knocked off its axis. Jeff saw Nettie as soon as he walked in the door and thought she was prettier than prairie flowers. He wanted to speak to the girl but was afraid and kept shifting from one foot to the other, fighting his fear of rejection. Finally, he mustered the courage to approach her and introduced himself. He explained that he lived on a farm about fifteen miles outside Bolivar with his parents and rarely came to town. He was in the dry goods store today because he was running low on cartridges for his rifle.

As Jeff was talking, Nettie was looking him over and liked what she saw. He was tall, nearly 6' 2" in his stocking feet, with long curly, well-maintained blond hair. The young man was sturdy and obviously strong with a commanding voice and quick laugh.

Jeff tried to engage Nettie in conversation, but at first, she seemed a little standoffish, though not rude. Jeff explained that he didn't know much about girls; heck, he didn't even have a sister. He went on to explain that he thought Nettie to be a very handsome girl and would like to call on her if she would be inclined to allow a visit.

Jeff walked Nettie out to her buggy, carried her purchases, and helped her climb into the buggy. Jeff and Nettie talked for a few minutes, and she explained that she enjoyed talking to him but had to get started back home to fix dinner for her father who stopped work at 4:30 PM. He liked to eat dinner after smoking a bowl of pipe tobacco and having a couple fingers of bourbon.

Nettie looked at Jeff and smiled. "If you really want to come court me, we eat at 6:00 PM. Please come this coming Friday evening and be prompt." Nettie gave Jeff directions to her home and informed him that her father was the Circuit Judge. She told Jeff that he shouldn't be intimidated. Her father was a stern man and protective of his only child, but he would warm up a mite after he had time to appraise Jeff. With that bit of forewarning, Nettie and Jeff bid each other good day.

Jeff showed up at the Strong house at precisely 6:00 PM Friday evening and was met at the door by Nettie. She welcomed him into the house and took him directly to her father. Judge Strong was having a glass of bourbon while sitting in his rocker in front of the fireplace. The judge looked up when he saw Nettie and the young man approaching and stood.

Jeff held out his hand and said, "Hello, Sir, my name is Jeffrey Blake Spencer, and I live with my parents on a farm outside Bolivar."

Bart looked the young man in the eye and replied, "I know your father, and John Spencer is a good man."

Jeff agreed that his father was honest and hardworking, and he hoped he would prove to be as worthy of people's respect. Nettie took off for the stove and left Jeff and the judge to talk for a few minutes. The supper was great with a nice pot roast and Judge Strong's favorite, apple pie, for dessert. Nettie was pleased to learn apple pie was also Jeff's favorite.

After dinner Nettie cleaned off the table and placed the dishes in the sink to be washed later, and she and Jeff walked out to the porch and sat on the swing and talked until Judge Strong tapped his pipe on the fire box and said, "Tomorrow is a new day. Time to get some rest now."

Jeff became a fixture at the Strong home. Judge Strong wondered to himself if he needed to get a part-time job to help offset the growing grocery bills. After a few weeks, Jeff took Nettie to meet his parents, John and Mary Spencer. She was greeted warmly by Mrs. Spencer and courteously by Jeff's father.

On the first day of February 1871, Jeff went to the Polk County courthouse and asked to see Judge Strong. The judge was in his chambers smoking his pipe and relaxing. He greeted Jeff and asked him to sit down. Jeff began talking about the weather and how the early grass was coming along on the farm. Then he started talking about maybe going fishing the coming weekend.

Judge Strong looked at him and said, "Son, why don't you just spit out whatever it is you came here to talk to me about?"

Jeff turned red and said, "Sir, I want to marry your daughter. I will take care of her and provide a home for her if I can receive your blessing."

Judge Strong turned his swivel rocker to face away from Jeff and looked out the window and played with his pipe as tears started forming in his eyes. He knew this day was coming as soon as he had seen how Jeff and Nettie looked at each other. But he wasn't ready for his only child to marry and leave home. In his mind, Nettie was still his little girl and certainly not ready to marry.

When he turned around to face Jeff, he looked him directly in the eyes and said, "I don't think Nettie could do better. You are a fine young man. What are your plans?"

Jeff explained that he had been working on other farms when his work on the Spencer farm was done. He had been saving his money since he was thirteen years old and had put aside enough to make a fair down payment on a 400-acre tract in Hall County, Texas. He went on to explain that the agent he had contacted in Texas had assured him that water was plentiful, the soil good, and that the land was ideal on which to raise longhorn cattle.

Judge Strong was taken aback and thought silently that this young man was asking a lot. First, he wanted to marry his only child, and now he was telling him he wanted to take her hundreds of miles away to a place full of hardships and wild Indians. He wondered if the young man had any other good news. He soon discovered there was more.

Jeff told Judge Strong that he would like for he and Nettie to be married fairly soon because he needed to build a house for them before the harsh Texas winter set in. He went on to say that he had been informed that Texas winter winds could be mighty tough even with a solid house to keep you warm.

Judge Strong expressed his concern regarding the Comanches which were still in that part of Texas and asked Jeff how he intended to protect Nettie. Jeff assured Judge Strong that he was a better than fair shot with a rifle and intended to teach Nettie to shoot. Judge Strong was filled with trepidation but gave Jeff his blessing.

Jeff and Nettie were married on the 4th of July 1871. Jeff was nineteen, and Nettie was eighteen when they climbed into the farm wagon leading a saddle horse and a milk cow and headed for Hall County, Texas.

Bart Strong was a practical man. Some fathers would have given a piece of furniture or perhaps a set of china as a wedding gift, Bart opted for matching 1866 Winchester Yellow Boy rifles in .44 Henry rimfire. The Yellow Boy held fourteen cartridges, was well constructed, and the lever-action allowed a shooter to fire several times without reloading. Along with Jeff's Henry rifle, they would be well armed.

Chapter 7

Jeff and Nettie Spencer's small ranch was situated on a slight plateau in a valley by the Prairie Dog Town Fork of the Little Red River in the rolling hills of Hall County, Texas. Hall County was named such in honor of Warren D. C. Hall, who was Secretary of War for the Republic of Texas. The soil was a mixture of red and black sandy loam, and the Little Red supplied ample water for cooking, bathing, washing clothes, and for the future cattle and other livestock needs. The rolling hills provided plenty of grass for cattle, and the fertile soil made for a great garden spot which Nettie took great pride in.

Once they arrived, Jeff got to the task of building a small pole corral for the horse which could be enlarged when needed for the addition of more horses. He then began work on a house. It wasn't to be anything fancy, just a sod building to keep the rain and cold out and provide a small measure of creature comfort. The rolling prairie would supply plenty of thickly thatched sod for the house, and there were enough trees to supply the timber needs for the roof trusses. While Nettie was hoeing an area the cabin would sit on to rid it of grass, Jeff began the project of cutting sod into bricks and began stacking them in an overlapping fashion to form the walls. Nettie continued to work the soil and smooth it and packed it as best she could by adding a little water and then smoothing the surface with a broom.

The house was small; perhaps twenty by twenty feet square with walls about seven feet tall on the front and sloping to about six feet six inches on the back to allow for drainage. There were enough cedar and hackberry trees to supply the poles for roof trusses, a door, window shutters, table and chairs, and a bed. After securing the roof poles, Jeff cut more sod bricks and placed them to make a watertight roof. The sod cabin was rustic, to say the least, but warm and dry. There were slots in the door to allow shooting at attackers if necessary, and three small windows, one on the front and one each of the two sides. They could be opened for ventilation and when closed provided shooting openings. Jeff had built a fireplace and flue which drew well and let the smoke escape. It wasn't elegant, but it was a start.

The Spencers were the first to settle in Hall County, Texas. The Apaches were still causing mischief in the area but never bothered them and were being forced out by the Comanches which were far worse. The threat of Comanches would be with them for almost four years until the Red River War of

47

1873–74 after which, the hostiles were forced onto a reservation in 1875.

****

The Red River War was a military campaign launched by the United States Army in 1874 to displace the Comanches, Kiowas, Southern Cheyenne, and Arapaho Indians from the Southern Plains, and forcibly relocate the tribes to reservations in Indian Territory.

****

Jeff's next order of business was to take a horseback trip to the Charles Goodnight ranch in Palo Duro Canyon near Amarillo, Texas.

****

Charles Goodnight, also known as Charlie Goodnight, was an American cattle rancher in the American West, perhaps the best known rancher in Texas. He is sometimes known as the "father of the Texas Panhandle." He never learned to read or write, but had his wives write letters for him to various individuals, including Quanah Parker.

48

****

Jeff didn't want to leave the milk cow alone on the spread for fear it might wander off or be stolen, but he certainly wasn't going to leave Nettie alone. So he took her into Memphis, Texas, and left her in Mollie Bearden's boarding house while he went to see Mr. Goodnight. He had no idea if Mr. Goodnight would even receive him, let alone help him or give him advice, but he knew he would need both to build an effective ranch in the rough Texas hills.

The trip to the Goodnight ranch was about 85 miles and took two days and nights on the trail. Jeff arrived around noon on the third day. Blackie, his black stallion with a white face, made the trip like he was just out for a leisurely afternoon trot. When Jeff rode up to the Goodnight ranch house, he was greeted by a solid looking man who announced he was the ranch foreman. He advised Jeff he didn't need to get down off his horse because they weren't hiring drovers. Jeff thanked the man for the information and told him he wasn't looking for work, but he was hoping to speak with Mr. Goodnight for a few minutes.

At that point, a large man with coal black hair and long beard appeared on the porch and said, "Who is it that wants to see me?"

"Sir, my name is Jeff Spencer, and I have purchased 400 acres in Hall County and have it in my mind to build a cattle ranch."

Goodnight took the measure of the young man before answering and then said, "Why in the hell would you want to live on the prairie and raise dumb, ornery longhorns? Don't you have enough problems without inviting more?"

Jeff turned red in the face, fidgeted in the saddle, and replied, "With all due respect, Sir, you are no doubt smarter than me, and you raise longhorns."

Goodnight bent over laughing and, when he straightened up said, "Boy, you got me there. You've got more grit than sense. Come on in the house."

Jeff stayed a week on the Goodnight ranch, worked for his keep, and bunked with the ranch hands. Leslie Stevens, Goodnight's foreman, took Jeff under his wing and showed him everything that could be packed into a week on the ranch. Jeff learned about designing a branding iron and how to use it, how to soothe cattle to keep them calm, how to detect and treat some of their more common ailments and got some useful information on selective breeding techniques. Stevens told him right off if he had a deficient bull, he needed to have it for dinner because it would contaminate and weaken the entire herd. Jeff thought he knew about cattle because he had tended to milk cows on his dad's farm, but this was a whole new kettle of fish. These weren't docile milk cows. These critters could kill you if you got the slightest bit careless and could disembowel a horse with one sweep of their horns. A full-grown longhorn steer could have horns as wide as seven feet, tip to tip, and some were rumored to have been as much as eight.

On the last night on the ranch, Charles Goodnight invited Jeff in the house for dinner and asked him, "So, do you still want to go into the cattle business?" Jeff allowed he did and wanted to know if he could purchase a bull and heifer from the Goodnight herd.

Without any hint of ceremony, but with no trace of harshness, Mr. Goodnight said, "No, you can't. I will see you in the morning before you leave, Mr. Spencer." With that dismissal, Jeff thanked Mr. Goodnight for an excellent meal and all the help his foreman had provided during his stay, got up, and walked to the bunkhouse. Jeff was disappointed by Mr. Goodnight's refusal to sell him a bull and heifer but could not otherwise fault the man's kindness to him.

The next morning, Jeff roused out at daylight and went by the ranch house to say goodbye to Mr. Goodnight and thank him again for his kindness. When Jeff tethered his horse to the hitching rail, he looked up, and Charles Goodnight was standing on the porch looking at him.

Without a hint of a smile, Goodnight said, "Well, I guess the least a fool can do is help another damn fool kill himself. Come around the house with me."

When they walked around the house, there was a Mexican who looked to be about 100 years old holding rope leads attached to a fine-looking young bull and heifer.

Goodnight said, "Son, you are going to need some help to get started and a pair of longhorns for breeding stock. There are a lot of unbranded critters roaming the hills and prairies which have been running wild since the start of the Civil War. If you have the guts and grit to round them up and brand them, you will have the makings of a herd."

Goodnight went on to say, "Old Juan here doesn't look like much, but he has forgotten more about cattle than you and I know together. He will stay with you as long as you need him. Another gun won't hurt a thing either, once you get 'em you got to keep em.' Take the money you would have paid me for the cattle and invest it in firearms and cartridges. You are going to need them. And teach that pretty young wife you keep talking about how to shoot and shoot well. You folks are on your own, and the Comanches will think you are easy pickins until you show them otherwise."

Jeff thanked Mr. Goodnight profusely and shook his hand. As Jeff Spencer rode off, Goodnight stood on the porch watching the young man head down the trail. Leslie Stevens walked up and said, "I hate to see that boy leave. He is a fine young man."

Goodnight agreed and replied, "Yep. If I had been fortunate enough to have a son, I would be proud if he were like that young man. I hope he keeps his hair. Have a drover stop in and check on him when they are out his way checking stock."

The trip back took four days and three nights on the trail because they didn't want to wear down the bull and heifer. They made cold camps each night so they wouldn't leave a smoke signal for Indians to detect. About noon on the fifth day, Jeff and Juan Gonzalez walked their horses into Memphis, Texas, leading a bull and heifer. They stopped at the boarding house and were greeted by a very happy Nettie. After making introductions of Juan to Nettie, Jeff got her mare from the livery, and they started home to the ranch. Before leaving town, Jeff drew a sketch of a brand he wanted the blacksmith to make for him, a "J" within a circle. His would be the Circle J brand. He told the blacksmith he would pick the branding iron up in a few days.

Jeff had the extra money he had planned to spend on the bull and heifer, so he went to the mercantile store and purchased a Colt Navy pistol which had been converted to fire the new .38 rimfire cartridge. He got a gun belt and cross-draw holster, fifty rounds of .38 and 300 rounds of .44 cartridges. He wasn't expecting trouble, but it paid to be prepared.

Jeff and Juan spent their days rounding up cattle from the hills, thickets, and sage tangles and driving them back reasonably close to the sod house. Jeff left Juan with some work to accomplish and rode into Memphis and picked up the branding iron. He didn't want to get many cattle bunched up before he started the branding process. After a couple months of backbreaking work, Jeff and Juan had gathered about fifty head of cattle and caught five mustangs. Jeff and Juan had built a crude sod shelter for Juan with a forge under an overhang on the side nearest the corral. While Jeff went into Memphis to retrieve the branding iron, Juan began to fit the mustangs with iron shoes.

Jeff returned with the branding iron, and the next morning he and Juan began branding the cattle and mustangs they had gathered. After all the livestock were branded, Jeff began the process of saddle breaking the mustangs.

On July 4, 1872, Nettie presented Jeff with a very healthy and loud daughter they named Mary Lea Spencer. Mary after both her grandmothers and Lea after her mother. On June 10, 1873, Nettie gave birth to John Barthelme "Little Bart" Spencer who was named John after both grandfathers and Barthelme after Nettie's father.

Juan stayed with the Spencers and helped Jeff with every facet of ranching. Within two years, filled with backbreaking work, Jeff and Juan had built up a herd of about 250 Texas longhorn cattle, and Jeff Spencer had acquired enough cattle knowledge to call himself a cattleman.

Chapter 8

On the morning of July 13, 1874, Jeff awoke to the sound of horses neighing in the corral. When he looked out the shooting slot in the door, he saw five Comanches fixing to open the corral gate to steal the horses. Jeff opened the door and took aim with his rifle. Juan appeared at the opening of his quarters with his Spencer at the ready.

Jeff hollered to the Indians, "Don't open the corral. Get back on your horses and ride off." The Comanche who had his hand on the top corral pole looked at Jeff with a look of complete hatred and jerked the pole loose from its slot. Jeff shot him in the chest with a .44 caliber slug from his Winchester repeater. One of the other four Comanches jumped on his pony and charged the house. Juan dropped him in the yard with a single shot. The remaining three Comanches got on their horses and headed for the hills. In less than 30 seconds the battle with the Comanches was over. The Indians hadn't managed to get off a single shot. Two were dead, and the other three were heading for the hills. Unfortunately, the initial confrontation with the Comanches was just the start of a long few days.

After the Indians left, Jeff went out and pulled the two bodies off on the far side of the corral. He didn't know anything about the Comanche burial customs and figured they would return for the bodies at night.

When he got finished moving the dead bodies, he walked back to the cabin. Juan met him and said, "Señor Jeff, I would suggest that we fill some buckets with water and gather fire wood. I don't think the Comanches are gone."

"I hope you're wrong, but I see the logic in what you say." Jeff and Juan gathered water from the creek in every container they could find and cut ample firewood for a few days if it was used sparingly.

Slightly after 1 PM, Bill saw somewhere around fifty Comanche Indians assembled across the creek from the cabin. "Well, Juan, it seems you were correct, but I wish you had been wrong. You've fought these Indians, what can we expect?"

"Señor Jeff, they will not be foolish like the five who came this morning. I think they will try to steal the horses and set fire to the cabin."

Jeff had a Winchester standing against the door, another by the left window, and the Henry at the right window. They were as prepared as they could be.

The first attempt by the Comanches was to get the horses from the corral as Juan had guessed. Two Indians came up to the corral on foot and went to the gate. Jeff took aim and fired at the nearest Indian and hit him in the upper leg. He went hobbling off with the second Indian helping to support him.

Right after 4 PM, the Comanches began a barrage of rifle fire at the cabin. Based on the number of shots, Jeff figured the Indians had Henry or Winchester repeating rifles. Jeff, Juan, and Nettie got on the floor as the bullets hit the door and windows. The children were in the corner of the cabin behind a bed mattress. After a minute or so the firing stopped, and all was quiet. The first day of the Comanches' attack was over.

Just after daylight on the 14th, the Indians began randomly firing at the cabin door and windows. Jeff looked out the shooting opening on the door and saw two Indians headed on foot to the corral. He took aim, fired, and the nearer of the two Comanches went to his knees. The other Indian began dragging the wounded warrior and two other Comanches suddenly appeared and helped with getting the wounded man back to safety.

While he was watching the Comanches drag the wounded warrior off a bullet came through the opening on the door and hit him in the left shoulder. Actually, the bullet went through the meaty part of his shoulder just above the clavicle. He was lucky. Beyond bleeding and hurting like the dickens, it wasn't a life threating wound.

Nettie saw all the blood and came over and helped Jeff get his shirt off. There was a small hole in the front and a much larger hole in the back of his shoulder where the bullet had exited.

"Nettie, we've got to get the bleeding stopped. Get the poker, put it in the fire, and when it gets really hot put it on the place where the bullet came out."

"I'll heat the poker, but I don't know if I can burn your wound with it."

"Nettie, we're on our own out here. If we're to survive, we'll have to do a lot of things that aren't pleasant. Juan could do this, but he may not be around next time, so I want you to do it."

Reluctantly, Nettie took the hot poker and placed the tip against the site where the bullet exited. The smell of the cooking tissue was sickening but she got the blood vessels cauterized.

Jeff had placed four boxes of .44 rimfire ammunition on the table. He hoped that they wouldn't need anything close to that amount but there was no way to know. He had several more boxes of ammunition in reserve, but, so far, he had only fired three times. He didn't think that lack of ammunition was going to be the problem.

The remainder of the day the Indians fired just often enough to remind the Spencers and Juan that they were still around.

Nettie looked at Jeff and said, "We have enough food for four or five days. Do you think we'll be able to wait them out?"

Jeff laughed and replied, "Since they have all the cattle they want to eat, we just have to hope they get enough of the waiting and go back home."

On the 15th, the third day of the siege, the Comanches tried another tactic. As the sun peeked over the eastern horizon three Comanches came towards the cabin with the rising sun at their backs as fast as their horses could run.

Jeff was at the east window and saw movement when the Indians began their charge. It was very difficult to get a good sight alignment while looking into the bright sunlight, but Jeff got off five shots before they got to the cabin. One warrior was on the ground, one horse was down, and the rider injured from when his mount had rolled over him, and the third wasn't in Jeff's view. He heard a horse snort and realized that the hostile was in a blind spot beside the cabin.

"We've got a problem. One of the Indians is right beside the cabin. The walls are around ten inches thick, so he can't get in that way. If he tries to shoot in through the windows or door, he will expose himself. I think he will get on the roof and try to get in through the logs."

As the day progressed, nothing was heard from the Indian who was beside the cabin. He would have to stand on his horse to get on the roof and Jeff hadn't heard any noise from the roof. There was the occasional rifle shot which hit a window or the door, otherwise nothing of consequence happened.

When it got close to sunset, Jeff turned to Juan and said, "Cover the east window please. I'm going to go out and see what's going on with the Indian beside the cabin as soon as it gets darker."

In a few minutes, the sun set behind the western horizon and Jeff pulled his Colt Navy revolver and eased out the cabin door. He kept his back against the cabin wall and slowly made his way to the corner. He took a deep breath, stepped around the corner, saw an Indian sitting on his horse, and fired his pistol. The Indian fell off his horse and wriggled on the ground in obvious pain. The bullet had hit the hostile in the thigh. Whether it went completely through was unknown.

Jeff had a decision to make. He could either kill the Indian, try to get him on his horse so he could ride back to his group, or take him inside and see about tending to his wound.

The Indian's rifle was on the ground. Jeff walked over, pulled the hostile's knife out of its sheath and flipped it out of reach. It looked like the bullet had hit a vein because the Indian was leaking a lot of blood. Jeff put his arm under the Indian's armpit and helped him limp into the cabin.

Nettie was scared to death of the Indian and Juan was suspicious at best. Jeff laid the hostile on the floor and examined his wound. The bullet was still inside the man's leg.

"Heat up that poker again, Nettie. I need to get this bleeding stopped." Jeff held hard pressure against the bullet entry site and the bleeding stopped within a few minutes.

Nettie walked over with the hot poker and handed it to Jeff. He handed the Indian a large rag to bite down on and signaled what he was about to do. The Indian just looked at him. The Comanche didn't even grunt. Jeff put some horse salve on the site and bound the leg with a length of cloth and tied it off.

Jeff helped the Comanche up off the floor, supported him as they walked to his horse, and helped him onto the animal. He picked up the Indian's rifle, ejected all the shells, picked up the knife, and handed both to the hostile.

The next morning when the Spencers and Juan looked out of the windows and door, all the bodies had been removed, and the Indians appeared to be gone.

Other than the carcass of a cow that the Comanches had killed and cooked while they were trying to wait the Spencers out, they suffered no losses.

Once in a while Jeff would see the tracks of a cow and a few unshod ponies leading the animal away, but the Comanches never attacked them again.

Chapter 9

The sun rose on the 17th of May, 1879, just as it had for millions of years. Nettie was washing the breakfast dishes and trying to keep her two wild Indians under control.

Jeff and Juan had just finished their morning coffee and gotten an early start on the day's activities. Jeff was saddle breaking a dun colored mustang, and Juan was repairing a shoe on a gelding when the riders came into the ranch yard. They went unnoticed by the two men who were preoccupied until one of the riders rode up to the forge and pulled a shotgun. Juan reached for his rifle and was cut down by a shotgun blast. Nettie heard the shot and grabbed one of the Winchesters from the rack over the door. She cracked the door and saw Juan lying in a pool of blood and then, to her horror, saw the men shooting Jeff. She took aim at a large redheaded man holding a Sharps carbine and pulled the trigger. The impact of the bullet jerked the man off the saddle and onto the ground. Before she could select another target, a large, filthy hand jerked the rifle from her grasp.

The men pulled their horses up to the hitching rail in front of the house and dismounted. The filthy hand holding Nettie belonged to a half-breed whose hair was arranged in side braids. The men seemed disinterested in their friend who was lying on the ground, gut shot, and screaming for help. The six men were focused on Nettie. The six men had their way with Nettie. When the pain and humiliation was over, they killed the young woman. The little boy and girl were huddled in a corner of the cabin, terrified and crying. The men began a discussion on what to do with the children.

Charles Daile told the group "I want no part in killing children!"

Weathers knew the boy and girl would give a fair likeness of them to the local sheriff. After what they had done to the children's mother, a wanted poster with a likeness of each of the six men would be on every jailhouse wall in the west. Since abusing and killing a woman was taboo even amongst the hard men of the west, they would be shot on sight. Weathers pulled his Bowie knife and cut the throat of both children and turned and walked out of the cabin without the slightest sign of remorse.

The men began rounding up the horses from the corral and driving the cattle nearest the ranch towards the northeast. As they went along, they gathered more cattle until they had about150 head of the herd Jeff had built. In about thirty minutes, the men were out of sight and headed towards Oklahoma Territory, hopefully to find a buyer who had little interest in brands or who they could convince the Circle J was their brand.

Two range riders from the Goodnight ranch were roaming the southwestern section of the giant ranch looking for stray cattle and were riding to the Spencer ranch when they heard several gunshots. They figured the shots were nothing more than Jeff and Nettie Spencer doing a little target practice. Foreman Stevens had reminded them that Mr. Goodnight would want a report on the Spencers. Even though the gunfire was a couple miles off, they decided they should hurry on over to the Spencer ranch which was in the direction of the shots. They spurred their horses to a gallop, going to satisfy their curiosity and satisfy Stevens more than anything. When they got to the ranch, they were presented with a ghastly sight.

Men who lived on the Texas frontier were accustomed to death, rattlesnakes, swollen rivers, bar fights, cattle stampedes, disease, and the occasional knife or gun fight; each of which extracted a toll on humanity. But nothing they had ever seen prepared them for what they encountered when they rode into the yard of the Spencer ranch. Old Juan was lying in a splayed position next to the

66

forge with most of his head gone, obviously the result of a shotgun blast from fairly close range. Jeff Spencer was in the horse corral, dead as the result of several gun shots to his torso. A red-headed man was leaning against the corral fence with two bullet holes in him, one to the gut and another between his eyes.

As bad as the sight of the three men was, nothing could have prepared them for the carnage in the ranch house. The cabin looked like a slaughter house with blood everywhere. Even for the hard Texans, the sight of the dead children brought tears to their eyes. What type of animals would do something like this? The cowboys carried Jeff and Juan into the cabin and laid them on the floor, placed Nettie and the children next to them, and covered the bodies with blankets from the beds.

One drover lit out for Memphis to let the sheriff know what had happened, and the other headed for the Goodnight ranch to report what they had found to Mr. Goodnight. When Hall county sheriff, Wade Russell, received word of the killings, he ordered a farm wagon prepared to go to the Spencer spread and retrieve the bodies. He then walked towards the telegraph office dreading the message he would have to send:

"Judge Bart Strong, Bolivar, Missouri (Stop) Nettie, Jeff, children killed by persons unknown (Stop) Advise funeral arrangements (Stop) Wade Russell, Sheriff, Hall County, Texas."

The message was delivered to Judge Strong within a few minutes after it arrived at the telegraph office, and he replied after recovering from the shock:

"Sheriff Russell, Memphis, Texas (Stop) Bury family church cemetery Memphis (Stop) Be your location ten days (Stop) Bart Strong."

Judge Strong had feared something like this would happen, but his fear had been of Apaches and then Comanches. After the hostiles were subjugated and moved to reservations, he figured the land would be safe, and his daughter and her family would enjoy a long and prosperous life. As it turned out, their lives were short and ended brutally.

On a whim in 1876, Judge Strong had purchased one of the new-fangled Smith & Wesson Schofield Model 3 .45 Colt revolvers from a gun salesman who was traveling through Bolivar and carried it to court every day. He would take the pistol outside of town and practice about once a week. The problem was a box of 50 .45 Colt cartridges cost almost as much as the weapon itself. After a few trips to practice, Judge Strong decided he could shoot the revolver or eat, but not both.

He still worked with the pistol but only aimed and dry fired the weapon.

About once a month for many years, Judge Strong had taken out his Greener double barrel shotgun and the Whitworth .451 caliber rifle he carried throughout the Civil War, wiped them off with an oil rag, and cleaned the barrels. He now got them both out. After going by the dry goods store and buying some bacon and beans, Arbuckle coffee, a box of bullets for the revolver, two boxes of 00 buck shells for the Greener, lead to make bullets, powder charges, and primers for the Whitworth, Bart Strong had his supplies ready for his departure.

Bart Strong was no longer a young man. He was sixty-three years old when he received the news of Nettie and the rest of his family. He still had his hair, albeit more of it was gray rather than the dark brown of his youth, and most of his teeth. He was fairly tall at five feet eleven inches in height and weighed about 200 pounds, twenty pounds heavier than when he went on the bench. He had a large mostly gray moustache and shaved every day. Bart had a strong jaw, steel grey eyes, and rarely smiled. Strong was fashion conscious and typically wore light colored trousers, a brown frock coat, and low-cut vest. When preparing for this trip to Texas, Bart exchanged his Bowler for a brown Stetson slouch hat with a two-inch brim, his frock coat for a Mackinaw, and bought a pair of Coffeyville style boots to replace his ankle high lace-up shoes. Thus attired, Bart was ready for horseback travel and tracking the killers of his family.

Judge Strong knew he really didn't have any jurisdiction over the crimes in Texas, but he decided to write several John Doe execution orders for murder convictions in absentia. The writs weren't really worth the paper they were written on, but he doubted any lawman was going to question them. A writ for a rat wasn't gonna get much scrutiny. He placed the forms in a leather binder and put it in his haversack.

That night, while drinking a pot of coffee, Bart melted lead and molded fifty .451 bullets with his bullet mold.

Judge Strong placed everything on his docket on hold and informed Missouri Attorney General Jackson Leonidas Smith of the death of his daughter and her family and that he was going to Texas to settle their affairs and look for their killers. He advised Attorney General Smith he should appoint a replacement judge because he had no idea when or if he would return to Missouri. After three days, Judge Strong had done everything he could concerning pending trials and motions and packed his personal effects in his haversack. Before leaving, Judge Strong stopped in, made his goodbyes to his closest friends, and asked Jim Jameson, his childhood friend, to check on the house from time to time.

He put his saddle on the buckskin colored gelding he called Buck, secured the Whitworth in its scabbard, and tied it to the saddle. He then secured the panniers on the pack horse and placed his small skillet, coffee pot, food stuffs, blankets, and other items in the panniers. Bart then slipped the rawhide thong loop which was attached to the Greener around the saddle pommel, mounted the horse, and with the pack horse in tow, started towards Texas. He doubted he would ever see Missouri again.

Bart rode out of Bolivar on the 18th of May, 1879. He had told his old friend he would be in Texas in ten days. He found he was wrong on two counts: it was farther to Memphis, Texas, than he had figured, and his old body couldn't tolerate long daily rides. He arrived at Sheriff Russell's office just before noon on June 3rd, 1879.

Chapter 10

Wade Russell had served with Bart Strong under Bloody Bill Anderson and General Nathan Bedford Forrest during the Civil War, but they hadn't seen each other for more than fifteen years. Russell remembered Strong as a quiet man who kept to himself, not unfriendly, just solitary, thoughtful, and focused. Strong had few military duties in common with the soldiers on the line and would go out alone with his Whitworth rifle, strange looking spectacles, and binoculars. Strong would be gone for days at a time, and when he came back to the camp, he might talk to Wade for a few minutes. After a few weeks, Strong became more chatty and he and Russell became close friends.

Bill Anderson had seen Strong in a couple turkey shoots in Missouri during the late 1850s and remembered he could outshoot anyone and everyone with a rifle. In fact, hosts of turkey shoots began barring Strong from entering competitions because of his proficiency with a rifle. After the start of the Civil War, Anderson went to Bolivar, Missouri, and personally recruited Strong to serve with him in the guerilla group, Quantrill's Raiders, which was conducting raids on Union forces along the Missouri/Kansas state lines.

Strong's job was to go out alone and find a good vantage point from which to target Union officers and shoot them from long range. Being a sniper was a death sentence if caught by the enemy. Union soldiers and officers, in particular, hated men who could shoot them from great distances. Strong disliked killing and preferred to shoot the Union officers in the leg or shoulder when he could get an open shot. A wounded man tied up other men to take care of him, so it lessened the number shooting back at the Confederate soldiers by two or three. And it allowed the wounded man to return to his family; something which was a big priority with Strong.

After the war Strong got his hands on a set of Soule Vernier sights made by J. W. Soule of Boston, Massachusetts, and had a gunsmith install them on his Whitworth. The Civil War was over, but that didn't mean there wouldn't be another need for the rifle. The Soule sights could be adjusted both for elevation and windage and allowed him to hit an object at more than 1,000 yards away. The Whitworth rifle had a hexagonal barrel and shot the new elongated hexagonal shaped .451 caliber projectile, and the barrel had a 1 in 20 twist rifling which made the rifle extremely accurate. Where one pointed the Whitworth, it shot. During test firings in

73

England, the Whitworth held a 29" pattern at 1,100 yards. This was without the new Soule sights. Strong's longest shot during the war was about 800 yards and hit a Union colonel in the thigh.

In August 1863, Quantrill raided Lawrence, Kansas, killing 150 men and boys. Later in 1863, Anderson and Quantrill became embroiled in a dispute over some matter. Anderson took part of the group and returned to Missouri to wage a guerrilla war there. It was at that time Bill became known as "Bloody Bill Anderson" because of his ruthlessness. Strong was out on a reconnaissance mission during the Lawrence raid and Russell was home sick.

In September 1864, Anderson led his guerrillas to Centralia, Missouri, where they captured a passenger train. The Anderson bushwhackers killed twenty-four unarmed Union soldiers who were on the train. Strong was out on one of his sniper hunts at the time of the massacre. Russell had been relegated to a group as rear guard during the slaughter. After the incident, Strong and Russell had enough of the wanton killing and the likes of the James brothers: James Jason, James Liddil, and other cutthroats who killed for sport. Bart and Wade decided to leave the guerrillas and joined up with regular Confederate troops under the command of

General Nathan Bedford Forrest. While serving under Forrest, they participated in several engagements in Kentucky and Tennessee. Strong served the same function with Forrest as he had with Anderson: going out alone as a sniper to select Union officers to shoot. Russell was assigned to the cavalry, and he and Strong saw each other less frequently than when they were with the bushwhackers. Actually, Strong was attached to the unit of scouts under the command of Captain Bill Brubaker, so he could be better informed on Union troop locations and movements.

In April 1864, Russell and Strong again found themselves in the middle of a controversial massacre, this time at Fort Pillow on the Mississippi River in Henning, Tennessee. The battle ended with the slaughter of several Negro Union soldiers who were attempting to surrender. Again, Strong had been out on a hunting expedition for Union officers, and Russell had been in the medical facility having a musket ball removed from the muscle in his right thigh. But they both would always despise their association with the forces which committed the atrocities.

Russell and Strong maintained their friendship and served under General Forrest until the end of the war, at which time they bid each other a fond farewell and went their separate ways, promising to keep in touch.

Both men became lawmen, Russell in Texas and Strong in his native Missouri. Strong decided he wanted to practice law and ordered law books, studied them, applied to the Missouri Bar Association, and was accepted in 1870. Like many of those practicing the law in the 19th century, Bart Strong was self-taught. However, he never practiced law as an attorney for even a day and was elected Circuit Court Judge. He was seated in January 1871 and served in that capacity until he received notice his family had been killed in Texas.

Russell heard of Strong from time to time and got a couple letters through the years, but neither had seen the other again until Bart Strong rode into Memphis, Texas, leading a pack horse. Strong was sixty-four years old in 1879, and the inactivity of sitting behind the bench had caused him to put on a few pounds which settled in his girth. Strong was also coming to grips with the fact that the ground was much harder and uncomfortable than it had been during the war years. The one constant was that his eyes were the same, filled with resolve and now, hatred and lust for retribution. Bart had to wear spectacles to read a newspaper but still had the eyes of an eagle when focusing on distant objects.

Russell filled his old friend in on what he knew which wasn't all that much. A day before the murders, seven men had been seen by drovers from the Goodnight ranch. The men were returning to the Goodnight ranch after delivering fifty head of steers to an Indian reservation supply staging area just over the Texas border in Oklahoma Territory. The seven riders were about twenty miles northeast of the Spencer spread when they were seen. The drovers weren't close enough to make out the faces of the seven men, but they thought it strange they would be out in the desolate area with nothing between them and the Goodnight ranch but one small ranch. They had just assumed the men were headed to the town of Memphis, Texas.

The member of the gang who was shot by Nettie was named Bevis Smith who was a known associate of Buryl Weathers. Weathers was a cattle and horse rustler and cutthroat who traveled the eastern part of Texas, western Arkansas, and southern Oklahoma Territory looking for what he might be able to steal. The only other piece of possible information was six men had been seen driving a small herd of cattle and some horses towards Oklahoma Territory the day after the murders. This was far too coincidental to be mere chance.

Strong went to the barber shop, got his hair and moustache trimmed, paid for and enjoyed a bath, and got his clothes cleaned, or at least the first layer of dust removed. He then filled his pipe, lit it, and went to the jail to get Wade for an early dinner at the Mystic Café. As they ate and enjoyed their coffee, they reminisced about the war years and wondered how they could have been so near involvement with two famous Civil War massacres.

Russell asked Strong what he had in mind regarding the men who had killed his daughter and her family? Bart's response was about what he had anticipated, "I have been administering justice for the past several years, and I am going to impose fair punishment on those vermin, every man Jack of them. I have written death warrants for six John Does, and I will hound them to the gates of hell, if I must, to find them and rid the earth of them. I care not how long it takes or how far I must travel. I will kill them all."

To add bona fide accuracy to the warrants, Bart went to the telegraph office and sent his old Civil War acquaintance Texas Governor Lawrence Sullivan "Sul" Ross a message and asked him to issue John Doe warrants for the six men who had killed his family. The following day, a telegraph message arrived from Texas Attorney

General George McCormick, a fellow Confederate Civil War acquaintance, giving Strong authority to serve six warrants, dead or alive, for the killers of his family. Bart filed the telegraph message in his haversack with the warrants. McCormick had been a member of Wahl's Legion and was wounded at the Battle of Harrisburg, captured by Union soldiers, and lost a leg due to the injury.

Russell said "This ain't Missouri, Bart. This is a big, hard country filled with hard men. Once this bunch gets shut of the cattle and horses, they will mingle in with other killers. They could go to Brown's Hole in Utah or Hole-in-the-wall in Wyoming or dozens of other places where cutthroats, rustlers, and horse thieves congregate. You may encounter Black Jack Ketchum, Harvey "Kid Curry" Logan, or other men who will kill you simply because you represent the law."

Strong said without hesitation, "I have this to do."

Russel went on "Bart, you and I have to wear spectacles to read a newspaper. We have places that ache where we didn't know we had places a few years ago, and you are going up against men at least twenty years younger than you. They are all proficient with firearms and think nothing of killing. If you insist on doing this, I would advise you to either kill them at a distance with your Whitworth or up close with the Greener and before they can shuck a gun. If you try to be honorable and give them a chance, the buzzards will be feasting on you after the men pick your outfit clean. That's more talking than I have done all at once in ten years."

Bart's comment was "Thanks for the advice, Wade. I'll never find peace until I do this. I've lived a good life and have no family left, if I get killed, that is the price I will have to pay." After which he got up, shook hands with his old friend, and went to the hotel to get some rest before starting on his quest. It might well be the last decent night's sleep he would get for a long time and his bones could use all the pampering they could get. A soft bed was the ticket, at least for one more night.

Neither Wade Russell nor Bart Strong knew it at the time, but they were not to see each other again. Wade Russell, Civil War veteran, town marshal, and county sheriff would be killed by a drunk cowhand while trying to break up a bar room brawl in Memphis, Texas, in June of 1891. The absurdity of Russell's death was that the cowboy who killed him was shooting at someone else and hit the sheriff by accident.

Chapter 11

Six men had been seen driving what must have been Jeff and Nettie Spencer's cattle and horses headed towards Oklahoma Territory. Bart Strong and Russell had mutually figured the best place to start looking for the killers would be in Camp Supply, Oklahoma. Strong had been told by his old friend that thousands of head of cattle were driven through the Woodward County area of Oklahoma Territory each year, so there was a good chance that the Spencer cattle would be brought to that location to be sold for Indian reservation beef.

If Bart hadn't known it before he got on the trail from Missouri to Texas, he knew it after he completed the trip. He was no longer a young man. Realizing he wasn't on a timetable; Bart would ride an hour or so and then get down and stretch his legs. He would also stop a couple times a day, make a small fire, boil a pot of Arbuckle, and rest his bones. He favored aspen groves for his camp sites because they were self-pruning and would drop lower limbs in order to grow new ones farther up the trunk. There was always a ready supply of dry wood for kindling, and the white bark of the aspen would mask and help hide the smoke of a small campfire. As far as he knew, no one would be following or interested in him, but it was better to be cautious. After all, it wasn't Bolivar, Missouri.

The trail from Memphis, Texas, to Camp Supply, Oklahoma Territory, was about 175 miles. Bart took his time and made the trip in five days. He figured it was better to take his time, conserve his energy, and rest the horses and his old bones frequently so he would be fairly fresh when he arrived.

When Bart arrived in Camp Supply, his first stop was at the two saloons in the settlement to try to get some information. Bartenders tended to listen to drunken customers and normally knew most everything about what was going on in a town and the general area. If you could get them engaged in conversation, they would spill the beans on most anything. The bartender at the Lucky Lady Saloon told him Buford Thomas was the most likely cattle buyer to have purchased the cattle in question. Thomas was the agent for a large conglomerate in the East and was compensated on a commission basis on the difference between the purchase and selling price of the cattle procured. Because of his arrangement with his employer, if the price was right, he wasn't the greatest stickler for propriety of brands on the cattle he purchased.

When Bart approached Mr. Thomas, the cattle buyer was defensive. Strong assured him he had no interest in his business dealings beyond trying to find out if he had purchased some beef cattle with a Circle J brand on them. Thomas said he didn't remember any such brand.

Bart looked sternly at the cattle buyer and said, "Mr. Thomas, I'm tired, and I tend to be irritable when I get in that condition. My patience has been known to grow short, and sometimes I do impulsive things. Let's start over. Did you buy around 100 head of longhorn cattle with the Circle J brand on them a few weeks ago?"

Thomas looked defensive and responded, "Mister, I can't be expected to remember every brand I buy."

"Thomas, you are trying my patience. You have a tally book with the brands you purchased recorded. I don't give a hoot about the cattle per se. My interest is in finding the men who sold the cattle and who killed my family. You need to start talking, or you are about three seconds away from having a dent in your skull." With that Mr. Thomas got more cooperative and confirmed he had indeed bought ninety-seven head of beef cattle from one Buryl Weathers a couple weeks previously.

Bart thanked him and said, "Now we are getting somewhere. How many men were with this Weathers fella?" Thomas only admitted to remembering three other men and gave Strong their descriptions. Bart asked him if he had seen any of the men around the camp since the sale.

"I have seen the young kid in the Spotted Dog Saloon a couple times. As far as I know, he is still around the camp, but I don't keep tabs on him." Strong thanked Thomas for his help and bid him good day. The cattle buyer hustled off; no doubt happy to be away from the grumpy old coot.

After stabling Buck and the pack horse and washing up a might, Strong went to the only café in the camp and ordered a beef steak, fried potatoes, and coffee. He leaned his Whitworth, still in its scabbard, against the wall and rested the Greener in his lap. After eating his dinner and enjoying a couple more cups of coffee, he walked over to the Spotted Dog Saloon and took a seat at a table against a wall where he could see the bat wing door entrance. The saloon was very crude with dirt floors and sawdust spread liberally on the soil to absorb moisture from spilled drinks and tobacco leavings. Part of the wall was crude wood planks and the remainder was comprised of tent canvas. The bar was a series of wooden planks laid on top

84

of whiskey barrels. Strong ordered a beer, drank slowly, and waited and waited and waited. After about three hours, three beers, and three trips to the privy, he was rewarded by the appearance of a small young man with dirty blond hair and shifty eyes. The kid ordered a beer and engaged in conversation with another tough looking man at the bar.

Bart got up, left the saloon, went to the livery, saddled his horse, and affixed the bridle, lead, and panniers on the pack horse. He put the Whitworth and the saddle scabbard on Buck, the buckskin gelding, and tucked the Greener inside his duster. Bart went back to the saloon, hitched the horses outside, and went into the building. It was now about 9:00 PM and completely dark. The kid was still at the bar drinking beer and getting loud and obnoxious.

Around 10:00 PM, the kid started for the door, and Bart followed him out of the saloon, unhitched his horses, and walked them along the street keeping pace with the young thug. When they had gotten out of the light of the saloon and in nearly complete darkness, Bart called out to the kid, "Hey, can you tell me where a man can find a brothel in this camp?" The kid swaggered over and opened his mouth to give Bart the location when he was greeted with the barrel of Bart's S & W revolver across his skull. The kid went down like a fallen log. Bart picked him up with some difficulty and slung him on the pack horse. He quickly tied the killer's hands to his feet under the horse's belly and continued on down the street and out of town.

Bart held Buck to an easy trot for about an hour. When he found a likely camp site on a knoll at a copse of trees where he could see approaching riders for a couple hundred yards in three directions he stopped and made camp. He took the saddle off Buck, dumped the kid on the ground, took the panniers off the pack horse, and picketed both horses. The kid had awakened during the trip and was complaining about his head hurting. Bart assured him it would hurt a lot more if he didn't shut-up. Bart had the kid sit down at the base of a tree and tied his hands together behind the tree. Once he was satisfied that the kid couldn't get loose, he went about the task of making a small fire to brew a late-night cup of Arbuckle coffee. After relaxing for a few minutes and finishing his coffee, Bart turned in for the night. The kid started complaining about needing to pass his water, and Bart told him, "Go ahead, I'll see you in the morning."

At first light, Bart was awake, stoked the coals, and added some fuel to reheat his Arbuckle and fry some bacon. As he was cooking the bacon, he asked the kid, "What's your name?"

The kid smirked and responded, "The heck with you ole man. I'm not telling you nuthin."

Bart took a long, hard look at the kid and said, "Oh, you're going to tell me everything I want to know. It's just a matter of how much you want to hurt before you spit it out. Before this morning is over, you'll want to tell me things I don't even care about." With that, Bart continued cooking his bacon and drinking the Arbuckle. Strong took his time as if the world would wait for anything he might need to do. He finally looked at the kid and said, "Time to fess up, young fella. What's your name?"

The kid had been given lots of time to reflect on his situation and decided it would be best to tell the old man his name, "I'm called Slade Johnson."

"I already knew that, but now we are getting somewhere. Tell me the names of the men who were with you when you killed my daughter, her husband, and my grandchildren over in Hall County, Texas?"

Johnson blanched as white as snow, began swallowing, and lost his water. He began trying to formulate a lie which might get him out of his situation. "Mister, I was with them, I won't lie to you about that, but all I did was hold the horses. I didn't kill any of your kin and didn't molest the woman."

"Admittedly, I'm getting along in age and sometimes I forget things, but I don't remember telling you that my daughter was molested before she was killed? Look, Johnson, you are going to die today. Nothing is going to change that fact. I don't know if you personally killed my daughter, but you certainly were one of the men who raped her and did nothing to stop the killing. I have imposed a death sentence on you, and you will be executed today."

Johnson lost his bowels at the prospect of his impending death and began crying. "Please, Mister, I didn't hurt your daughter and had nothing to do with killing her."

Bart ignored his comment and asked, "What are the names of the five men who left the ranch with you? I know Bevis Smith was the man my daughter shot. I want to know the names of the other five men."

Johnson replied, "I ain't telling you nuthin more ole man."

Bart looked at the kid for a full minute and then said, "Oh, Johnson, you're gonna tell me everything I want to know. It just depends on how many toes you want on your feet when you die." With that, Bart took out his Bowie knife and slit Johnson's left boot from top to ankle, removed the boot, and threw it aside.

Strong then poured the last of the Arbuckle in his cup and leaned back against his saddle and gazed at Johnson. After a few minutes, he asked, "Ready to tell me their names, kid?"

"The heck with you," was the response. Bart took the filthy sock off the kid's foot, stuffed it in the boy's mouth, picked up his Bowie knife, grasped the kid's dirty foot, and cut off the little toe. The sun was starting to warm the air, and the kid was sweating profusely and smelled horribly from the urine and feces.

Strong looked at him and asked, "Looks like we are going to be here awhile. Do I need to make another pot of Arbuckle?" The kid had tears streaming down his face and shook his head side to side.

Bart removed the sock from the kid's mouth and asked, "What was that? Was there something you wanted to tell me?"

The kid hissed, "You ole coot, I don't deserve this!"

"You might be right; you probably deserve a lot worse. Are you ready with the names?"

"Yes, I'll tell you what you want to know. Why go through the torture, I don't owe them anything."

A few minutes later, Bart knew who the other killers were: Buryl Weathers, a half-breed named Cherokee Joe, Charles Daile, Wil Gabbage, and a gunfighter named James Smart.

Bart asked him where the men were headed, and Johnson said, "They told me they were going to Santa Fe, New Mexico."

Bart listened intently while he pulled a description of each man from the kid which pretty much agreed with Thomas's account of three of the men. Strong then saddled Buck, put the panniers on the other horse, and turned to Johnson.

The kid looked at him with pleading eyes and said, "I told you what you wanted to know. I don't want to die. Have mercy please."

Judge Strong looked at Johnson for a few moments and finally said, "My daughter, Jeff, and my grandchildren wanted to live too. You are guilty of rape and murder." And with that, he shot Johnson between the eyes with his S & W .45 and untied the kid's hands. A Colt .45 slug makes a real mess. Strong took no joy in snuffing out the life of the young man. On the other hand, if the man had been in his courtroom, given the evidence, he would have sentenced him to hang. A death sentence is a death sentence. Since there was no hangman around, it was merely his appointed duty as a servant of justice. He pulled the leather binder out of his haversack and wrote the name Slade Johnson on a warrant. He then dated and signed the warrant, put the form back in the folder, and placed it in his haversack. Strong then mounted Buck, took the lead of the pack horse, and rode off, headed southwest towards Santa Fe, New Mexico. One down, five to go...

Chapter 12

Strong figured the gang would want to stop, drink whiskey, and gamble away the money from the sale of the stolen cattle while riding to Santa Fe. Since some of Goodnight's wranglers might be in Amarillo and could possibly recognize them, they would find watering holes somewhere else. Dumas, Texas, seemed a likely spot. It had a company office for the railroad, a small hotel, general store, post office, and a saloon.

Bart realized that in his haste to get started, he had left Missouri with insufficient cash and would be running low on funds fairly soon. He knew a small place like Dumas wouldn't have a bank to receive a transfer. However, Dumas was along his route to Amarillo, so why not stop and see if one of the killers was holed up there.

Bart stopped in front of the Plains Saloon, hitched Buck and the pack horse to the rail, put the Greener inside his duster, and walked inside. He took a small table against the back wall of the room, ordered a beer, laid the Greener in his lap, and looked at all the men in the saloon. There wasn't anyone that fit the descriptions of the men in the room.

Bart was stretching out his legs and enjoying his beer when a dark haired man with an equally dark moustache walked up and said, "You have the smell of a law dog on you, Mister."

"I haven't had a bath in a few days, so I might smell like a lot of things."

"Are you sassing me ole man?" The men behind the talker started moving out of the line of fire just in case there was shooting.

Bart cocked the left hammer of the Greener and said, "Mister, you came over here for some purpose. Why don't you spit it out so I can finish my beer."

"I'm William 'Tulsa Jack' Blake and there's a reward on my head."

"Mister Blake, I've no interest in you or the reward money. Walk away."

Blake went for his pistol and Bart fired the shotgun. The load of buckshot hit the man in his right arm between his hand and elbow, and, for all practical purposes blew off his lower arm.

Bart looked at the bartender and said, "If you've got a sawbones in this settlement, you'd better get this man to him, otherwise he will likely get gangrene and be dead in a few days."

Blake was sitting on the floor mumbling to himself and was obviously disorientated and in shock. Bart walked by him, said, "I told you I had no interest in you," and continued out the door of the saloon, mounted Buck, took the lead of the pack horse, and headed for the Goodnight ranch in Palo Duro Canyon.

He decided to detour to Amarillo to have some funds wired from his bank in Bolivar, Missouri. He had met Goodnight during the Civil War and was impressed with the man. He later ran into Goodnight again while Charles was serving with the Texas Rangers and came to Missouri to pick up a prisoner to return to Texas for execution. As one gets older, friends tend to drift apart on the frontier or die off, so Strong decided to take the opportunity to visit with his old acquaintance while he was this close.

Strong stopped in Amarillo before going to the ranch, went to the Western Union office, sent a wire, hung around a saloon for a couple hours, and picked up some money which had been wired to the First National Bank. He then rode to the Goodnight ranch which was about twenty-five miles south of the town and arrived at dusk. Goodnight greeted Bart warmly, and they talked of Jeff Spencer and how much Charles had been impressed with the young man. In Goodnight's estimation, it was rare to find a young man so filled with ambition and determination and yet humble enough to ask for help. Goodnight told Bart about the time Jeff had called on him, worked on the ranch, and his gift to him of the bull and heifer and lending the old Mexican to help him build the ranch. Strong was touched, both by Goodnight's act of generosity and the loss of the young man who had married his daughter. Strong had thought of Jeff Spencer as his son, not just the young man who had married his daughter.

The two men commiserated and reminisced well into the early morning and consumed an entire bottle of bourbon in the process. Goodnight had his whiskey shipped in by rail and then coach from the Casper Company all the way from Winston Salem, North Carolina, and then had one of the drovers pick up the bottles two cases at a time in Amarillo. The bourbon was $.60 a quart plus shipping, expensive for the time, and more than twice the price of bar whiskey. It was far superior to the bar stuff, so why not indulge yourself if you had the money. Whiskey on the frontier could have most anything mixed in with the alcohol, and some was more useful for starting fires than drinking. John L. Casper built a million-dollar liquor business by selling mail order bonded whiskey.

Charles and Bart arose early and had a couple cups of coffee which did little to cure the pounding in their heads. Goodnight invited Strong to stay a few days. Bart declined, saying the men already had a head start, and every day put them farther away. Charles also offered the services of a couple of his hands who were very handy with a gun, but again, Bart declined. This was something he had to do himself, and he didn't want the responsibility of the lives of other men to contend with. Bart thanked Goodnight and said he would like to stay another day. He wanted to look at the cattle operation, and more importantly, let his head settle down before setting out.

Goodnight told Strong three of his hands had delivered thirty head of cattle to Dumas, Texas, just the week prior, and they stayed over one night in the hotel and visited the saloon. Everyone tended to know when killers were about, and the drovers hadn't heard any rumors of bad men while they were in Dumas. Goodnight had the men come to the ranch house, and Strong questioned them at length. The drovers couldn't remember seeing anyone who fit the descriptions Strong provided. Goodnight commented that Dumas was basically a railroad town in its early development and offered little which would appeal to the rougher crowd. Bart didn't mention that he had already visited Dumas and merely thanked Charles for the information. Bart decided to set out cross country towards Santa Fe, New Mexico. Bart got up early and had coffee with Goodnight. After saying their goodbyes, Bart rode off. Charles Goodnight had built the largest ranch in Texas and, along with John Chisolm, developed a cattle trail to Colorado. Strong and Goodnight's paths wouldn't cross again. Charles Goodnight would live to be an old man and die in Phoenix, Arizona, in 1929.

During the early afternoon of the day after leaving the Goodnight ranch, Bart stopped on a slight ridge overlooking the trail he had come down and built a small fire. He boiled a small pot of coffee, took the saddle off Buck and the panniers off the pack horse, and picketed them. Bart found a likely tree, leaned up against it, sipped on his coffee, and chewed on a bit of jerked meat. After a few minutes Buck's ears came up. He then neighed, and Bart picked up his Greener and laid it across his knees with the hammers cocked.

In a couple minutes, four riders trotted their horses into his camp and stopped. The older man of the group, without any greeting or ceremony, said, "We're trailing a man who stole one of my horses. Have you seen him?"

Bert replied "Nope. I've been here about an hour and haven't seen anyone but you folks coming or going."

"I'm Ike Truebud. I own the Circle T, and I think you're lying to me."

Bart looked sternly at the man and said, "I never heard of you, Mister Truebud, and I'm not fond of being called a liar. I told you I haven't seen anyone other than the four of you. That's the end of it."

"Mister, we hang horse thieves."

"That's interesting to know, Mister Truebud. Now can I get back to my coffee?"

One of the riders snickered. Truebud wasn't accustomed to people standing up to him and was obviously angry and embarrassed. Truebud said, "I've a good mind to hang you."

Strong calmly looked at the four men and said, "Well, there are four of you and only one of me, so you could get it done." He then looked directly at Truebud and said, "Mister Truebud, your problem is that you won't enjoy the hanging much because you will be dead."

Truebud looked at the Greener pointed at his ample gut, turned red, huffed, and they rode out. He hollered over his shoulder "I'll see you again." Bart hoped he never saw the grumpy old guy again and went back to his coffee.

During mid-afternoon of the sixth day on the trail, Strong stopped at the small trading post in Douglas, New Mexico. The little settlement had a primitive saloon, basically a tent attached to the side of the trading post. The bar consisted of boards on top of barrels. It was a perfect place to find the men Bart was looking for. The place was so rough and prone to shootings it would later be nicknamed "Six-Shooter Siding" when it took the name of Tucumcari. Strong tied his horses to the hitching rail, loosened the flank cinch on Buck and the pannier cinch on the packhorse, and pulled out his Greener. He placed the shotgun inside his duster, untied the scabbard, and tucked the Whitworth under his arm as he walked into the saloon. Bart found a seat at a small table, leaned the scabbard containing the Whitworth against the one other chair, ordered a beer from one of the saloon girls, and declined her offer of company.

As Strong surveyed the room he didn't see anyone who might be a significant loss to society if they were to be killed. But he was looking for five men in particular and had to be cagey in how he went about trying to identify them. There was a man who fit the description of one of the killers at a nearby table playing five card stud. After Bart watched the game for a half hour or so, he decided to ask to sit in and the men made a place for him. Strong introduced himself as

Bart Smith out of Amarillo, Texas, and waited for the names of the other players.

A large man wearing a black frock coat and black hat said, "We don't cotton much too using names here."

Bart looked the man over, and the interesting thing he noticed was that the man wasn't smoking or drinking. Bart smiled and replied, "No offense intended, Mister. I just like to know who I am playing cards with."

A shifty eyed man in a tattered coat and soiled hat spoke up and said, "I don't mind. My name is Charles Daile." Strong didn't bat an eye or twitch a muscle. He just looked straight ahead as if he hadn't heard the man.

The game consumed the afternoon and well into the night, with men getting out of the game and others filling the vacant seats. Finally, around 10:00 PM, Daile said, "I think I have had enough for today. I'm going to the hotel and get some sleep."

Strong got up and collected his meager winnings, tucked the Whitworth under his arm, and with the pistol grip of the Greener in his hand, followed Daile out of the saloon. Bart stopped and secured the scabbard containing the Whitworth on Buck and put the Greener under his duster.

Strong took a few strides, pulled out the Greener, cocked both hammers, and caught up with Daile in the middle of the street. Strong said, "Daile, you were part of a gang that killed my family in Hall County, Texas."

Daile started to plead, "I was with them, but I never laid a hand on your daughter and didn't kill anyone."

Bart replied, "You were there. You raped Nettie and did nothing to stop the killings. You have a shooter on your hip. I would fill my hand with it if I was you, but I'm going to kill you either way."

Daile looked Strong over and decided he had a fair chance because of the man's age, and as he thought about his prospects, his courage began to return. As he was contemplating going for his gun, Bart saw the change in his eyes and greeted it with a blast of buckshot from his Greener which opened a hole in the man's chest large enough to stick a fist in. The man was blown off his feet and flat of his back in the street.

Men started boiling out of the saloons and Bart loudly said, "This here is a personal matter. Daile was part of a gang that raped and killed my daughter and slaughtered my grandkids. I'm enforcing a murder warrant. I didn't want anyone in the saloon to get hurt, so I waited to settle this outside"

The men who congregated in Douglas were a hard lot, but killing a woman and

101

children was a heinous crime no one on the frontier would tolerate. The big man who had refused to give his name looked at Bart and said loud enough for all to hear, "My name is James Brown Miller, and if this piece of horse crap killed his kin, he had every right." Miller then turned to Strong and said in a loud voice, "No one here is going to bother you." And with that, the crowd began sauntering back into the saloons.

Miller looked at Strong and said, "Wish I had known what Daile done to your kin. I would have killed the jackal myself."

****

James Brown Miller, by his own admission, killed fifty-one men during his life. He was sometimes called Deacon Jim because he neither smoked nor drank and often attended church. Miller, aka Killer Miller, once one of the most ruthless killers and assassins of the old west, was lynched in Ada, Oklahoma, in 1909 after being acquitted of killing a U.S. Marshall. Obviously, the vigilantes took umbrage with the jury's decision.

****

Bart thanked Miller for interceding on his behalf, shook his hand, and went to the hitching rail. He retrieved the leather binder from his haversack, wrote the date, the name Charles Daile, signed the warrant, and replaced the folder. He then tightened the cinches on the horses, untied them, mounted Buck, and trotted the horses out of the camp.

After riding for about an hour, Strong stopped and made camp for the night. He brewed a pot of Arbuckle and reflected on his task. None of the men would have likely tried to settle Daile's score, but it was prudent to put some distance between himself and the town. When whiskey and guns were mixed, one might only be able to make the wrong assumption once!

Strong had started from Missouri in May. It was now late fall, 1879 and the nights were getting cold and the air crisp. The days were in the mid-50s. But at night, the temperature would dip into the low 30s, and it was only going to get colder. Bart wore a pommel duster over a heavy Mackinaw coat and was fairly comfortable during the day, but it was the nights which were starting to be a problem. It was obvious his old bones weren't adjusting to the cold weather. Bart had brought an extra bedroll and blanket. Still it was cold, miserably cold, at night. In Missouri he could sit by the fire at night. As miserable as the nights were, the weather wasn't his greatest concern. Winter was on the way and he was going to have to find a place to hole up til spring.

Judge Strong had taken on the role of executioner. He reflected on having administered justice on Charles Daile as he drank his coffee. Another one down and four to go…

Chapter 13

Bart was awake at sunup, got the fire going, warmed his hands, had his coffee and a bit of bacon. He saddled Buck, put the panniers on the pack horse, mounted, and walked the horses into the wasteland of New Mexico. He had about 250 miles to travel, and it was rugged country, only fit for fools, rattlesnakes, scorpions, cactus, and Apaches. Geronimo and his *Chiricahua* band were raiding small settlements, Mexican farms, ranches, and Indian pueblos. Interestingly, although not well-known due to dime novels and several mostly fabricated newspaper articles, Geronimo wasn't a chief; he was a medicine man. Because of his leadership abilities, he did have a fairly constant following of thirty to 100 men, women, and children at any given time and wreaked havoc in New Mexico, Arizona, and Senora.

Bart had been on the trail for about two hours when he came upon a small burned-out prairie house. The bodies of a man, woman, and two small children were lying on the ground outside the shelter. The man was scalped. The woman's dress was pulled over her head and her pantaloons had been ripped off. It took little imagination to figure out what the Indians had done to the woman before killing her. Bart rummaged around in a small out building and found a T-handle shovel. He selected a spot near a tree and began digging a hole large enough to bury all four bodies.

As he was digging, he heard the unmistakable yap and whine of a dog. He put the shovel down and started looking around to find where the sound had come from. He heard the whine again and realized the sounds were coming from the direction of the out building where he had found the shovel. He walked over to the small building, gazed in, and saw nothing but a scattering of tools and tack. As he turned to walk back to the grave site, he heard the whine again and walked around the building. When he peered around the back corner, he saw a mixed breed Saint Bernard. The dog was trying to move but had an arrow through its left thigh. Probably to satisfy their sense of humor, the Apaches had taken a hammer from the shed and pounded the arrowhead through the dog's leg and into the side of the building, immobilizing the animal. When they finished, they threw the hammer down by the dog.

Bart wasn't much of a dog lover, but he hated to see any animal suffer. He walked back to Buck and took the Greener off the saddle pommel and came back to the dog. Bart cocked the left hammer and aimed at the

106

dog's massive head. The animal just looked at him in a forlorn manner. "Darn, dog, why don't you growl and make this easier!"

Bart walked back to the pack horse and took a length of rawhide out of his haversack, went back to the dog, and said, "Dog, are you going to let me get you out of this mess or try to eat me?" The dog tilted his head, as only dogs can, as if he was trying his best to understand what the human was saying. Bart formed a noose and slipped it over the dog's muzzle, pulled it fairly tight, wrapped it again, and tied it off. He pulled his bowie knife and cut the arrow shaft, which was embedded in the building. He then grasped the end with the fletching, braced his knee against the dog, and jerked the shaft out of the animal. Bart stroked the animal's head a bit and talked to him for a few seconds. Then when the large dog seemed relatively calm, removed the noose, hoping the animal wouldn't tear him to bits.

Bart backed away from the dog cautiously, not knowing what he would do if the dog charged him, but at least it would be better to see him coming. The dog began wagging his tail and came up to Bart and brushed against him. Bart had some salve he had brought in case he or the horses should develop a saddle sore. He talked to the dog and placed some of the ointment on the entrance and exit sites of the arrow wound.

Bart went back to his grave digging, and the dog exhibited good sense and lay in the shade beside the house. Bart would work for a half-hour or so and then would join the dog in the shade and take a rest break before resuming his digging. It was reasonably cool, probably in the mid-50s, and the ground was mostly sand, so work wasn't terribly tasking. Finally, shortly before sundown, he had a hole large enough for a mass grave. He pulled the bodies to the hole and placed them in the grave in as dignified manner as possible. Bart said a few words out of the Good Book over them and covered the bodies with dirt.

Bart went to the tool shed and moved things around to make a place for his saddle and a pallet. He then made a small fire close to the shed door to heat some coffee, cook some bacon and beans, and warm his hands. He got a couple pieces of jerked meat out of his haversack and threw them to the dog. Two gulps and the pieces of meat were gone. After Bart had eaten, he walked to the shed and sat down with his back against the building, filled his pipe, lit it, and drank a cup of coffee. He threw the dregs of the coffee in the fire, went into the building and covered himself with his blanket. The giant dog came in and lay next to him on the floor.

Early the next morning, Bart got the fire going again, boiled more coffee, drank a cup, saddled Buck and got the panniers on the pack horse. After having a second cup of coffee, he drew some water from the well, rinsed out the cup, skillet, and coffee pot, and stored them in the panniers. After filling his two canteens, he threw another piece of jerked meat to the dog and covered the fire with dirt.

He started the horses west at a slow trot. About noon, he came over a slight rise and spied a ramshackle group of three buildings in a small valley and walked the horses up to the one which had horses tied to a hitching rail. He put the Greener in his duster and took the Whitworth and scabbard and walked into the dimly lit bar. After his eyes adjusted, he walked to a small roughhewn table by the back wall and sat down. The large dog trailed behind him and lay next to his feet.

A heavyset Mexican woman came to the table and asked what he would like. Bart responded, "A beer and some food if it is available." The woman walked off and came back with a bowl of peanuts and his beer and said they could cook him a beef steak. Bart told her that would be fine. As Bart looked around the room, he saw no one that met the descriptions he had of the men.

In a few minutes, a large man delivered his beef steak. Bart thanked him and asked the name of this place. The man responded, "Sugar Hill." Bart looked at him for a few moments and replied, "How did it get that name?"

"Well, ya see, my name is Fred Sugar, and I often asked myself why in Sam Hill I decided to stop here. So I named it Sugar Hill." Bart's curiosity thus satisfied, he lit in on the steak.

When Bart finished his food, he gave the steak scraps to the dog, and looked up and saw a man who was a walking oddity. Bart figured the man had been in the privy when he and the dog arrived because there was no way he could have missed this fellow. He was a tall man, perhaps more than six-foot-tall, with a giant slouch hat pulled down on one side and up on the other. He had on a fringed buckskin coat and matching trousers, not thrown together duds but well appointed by some tailor. The man had on thigh high boots that were well maintained and obviously custom made. The man had shoulder length dark hair, a large moustache waxed on the ends, and chin whiskers. His style of facial hair was known as a Van Dyke. As Strong was looking the man over, their eyes met, and the man walked over to his table.

He man opened a conversation by saying, "Good looking dog you got there."

Bart looked at the dandy for a couple moments and replied, "He ain't my dog." With that, the man reached down to pet the dog and was greeted by bared teeth and a low growl. Bart looked at the dandy, smiled, and said, "Guess he ain't your dog either."

The man looked at Strong and grinned, took off his right glove, stuck out his right hand, and said, "I'm Bill Cody and you are?"

Bart had kinda figured it was Cody because he had seen one of his Wild West show flyers in Missouri, and the likeness was apparent. Bart shook hands with Cody, introduced himself, and said "What the heck are you doing out here in the middle of nowhere?"

"I might ask you the same question, Mister Strong." Cody explained that he was between engagements with his show and had come to New Mexico in the hopes of influencing Geronimo to join his Wild West show. He went on to tell Bart that he had seen neither hide nor hair of the Apaches. In mid-sentence, Cody asked if he could sit down, and without waiting for a reply, took a chair and just kept talking and talking and talking. When Cody started yarning, the men in the saloon began to gather around to listen to his tales of buffalo hunts, Indian scouting for the army, and his time with the 7th Kansas Calvary during the Civil War. Cody stopped for a second and looked at Bart and asked, "Were you in the war?"

Strong smiled and replied, "Yep. Same place, probably at the same time. Different side, glad we didn't meet. I don't know if Geronimo was in the group, but I came upon some of his handiwork yesterday."

Cody smiled and said, "Yes, that would have been unfortunate for you had we met during battle. Are you sure it was Apaches that did this mischief."

"Well Mister Cody, I'm not an expert on Indians, but my understanding is that the Apaches are the only hostiles in this area."

Cody reflected on what Bart had said for a few moments and continued on with his stories. Bart sat in silence, or at least wished he could, while Cody just kept on blabbing and blabbing. Cody really wasn't bragging. He was just telling one story after another in rapid fire succession. After feeding the giant dog the steak scraps, Bart had given the large steak bone, with a degree of caution, to the dog. The giant canine gently took it from his hand and was still gnawing on it when Bart was ready to leave.

Bart finished his second beer and stopped Cody in mid-sentence. He apologized for needing to leave, extended his hand, and told him it was a pleasure to meet a genuine western hero, and that he had to get back on the trail. They shook hands, and Bart walked out of the saloon. The dog dropped what was left of the bone and walked at Bart's side as they exited the building.

****

William F. (Buffalo Bill) Cody was a legend in his own time. Cody started working at age eleven as a "boy extra" on a wagon train headed west and would ride a horse and deliver messages from one end of the train to the other. At fourteen, Cody was a Pony Express rider. At age seventeen, he was a teamster delivering supplies to the 7th Kansas Calvary during the Civil War. At age twenty-two, he was Chief of Scouts for the 3rd Calvary during the Indian wars on the plains. Cody received the Medal of Honor for his bravery during the Indian wars. The medal was revoked in 1913 because he was a civilian scout at the time of the award. His Medal of Honor was restored posthumously in 1988. While Cody was definitely a showman and unabashed self-promoter, he was without a doubt also a true western hero.

William F. (Buffalo Bill) Cody died on January 10, 1917, at seventy years of age.

The Buffalo Bill Center of the West in Cody, Wyoming, consists of five different museums and is well worth the time to visit.

****

Bart walked the horses away from Sugar Hill, up a slight incline, and started out into the grass filled plains towards the west. He rode until late afternoon and then settled on a likely place to make camp, took the saddle off Buck, the panniers off the pack horse and walked around for a few minutes. After resting his hind end and walking the kinks out a bit, he started a fire. While the pot of Arbuckle was boiling, he filled his pipe, lit it, and leaned up against a tree.

Right after Bart sat down, the big shaggy dog came and lay down beside him, nuzzled him on the arm with his nose, and looked at Strong with his big sad eyes.

****

The Saint Bernards are hunting, search and rescue, and watch dogs. They were brought into the Alps by the ancient Romans. The dog that Bart found left to die by the Apaches seemed to have a bit of some

114

other breed mixed in with Saint Bernard, but the animal still outweighed most men and could be very protective at times. Bart decided that calling the animal "dog" didn't seem respectful, so he chose Lucky because the animal was certainly lucky Strong came along and found him.

All in all, it had been a day to try to forget and a day to remember!

Chapter 14

Mid-morning of the third day after leaving Sugar Hill, Bart was ready for a change in diet. Eating nothing but bacon and beans while on the trail was pretty much a necessity. Bart liked beans well enough, but they gave him gas and made him fart like a pack mule. The weather was changing. It was now spitting snow, the winds were gusting, and the temperature seemed to be dropping by the minute. It was probably in the low 30s, but the wind made it feel like it was much colder. The wind and cold were coming right through Bart's Mackinaw and duster. Cold just affected older people more than the young. As Strong came over a slight rise in elevation, he saw a small spread below him in a valley. There was a wisp of smoke coming from the chimney, but the interesting thing was he didn't see any evidence of livestock other than a couple of horses in the corral.

Bart decided he would see if the occupants of the house would offer him a cup of coffee and maybe even a meal. He slowly and deliberately walked Buck down the incline while leading the pack horse.

When he got to within fifteen yards of the house, he hollered, "Hello, the house."

Nothing happened for a few moments, so Bart hollered even louder.

The cabin door opened slightly, and a rifle barrel appeared in the opening followed by a man's voice which said, "What are you wanting, Mister?"

Bart made sure both hands were exposed and replied, "I got caught in this gale and was hoping I could warm up a mite and maybe even get a cup of hot coffee, if it wouldn't be too much trouble."

"Hitch your horses to the rail and take off your gun belt and leave it and your shotgun on the saddle pommel and come inside. Walk slowly, and make sure I can see your hands. And that dog needs to stay outside"

Bart dismounted and complied with the man's instructions. Once inside, the man said, "Now open your duster, hold it up, and turn around."

Strong complied and saw a medium sized man with a large moustache and graying hair. The woman looked like most women of the west, aging before her time and tired. He took their two girls to be between twelve and fourteen years of age. Because he had raised a daughter didn't make him much of a judge of girls' ages. The cabin was lacking in refinement and only contained the necessities. The girls were clean but dressed in homespun dresses as was their mother. Bart introduced himself and sat at the table where the man pointed at an empty chair. Strong said, "You are kinda cautious with your entertaining."

The man exchanged the rifle for a Colt Navy revolver and introduced himself as Homer Jackson, originally from Austin, Texas. His wife was named Nellie May, and the girls were Joan and Jean. They had been on the small spread for five years and had managed to develop a small herd of about seventy-five longhorn cattle, five mustangs, and three milk cows. They had a large garden and raised most everything they ate. Everything was going reasonably well until they decided to attend a church revival.

The man explained they had traveled a day's journey to attend the church services in Santa Rosa, New Mexico. After the service, they had stayed overnight in the church. Because of the bitter cold, they didn't want to travel back to the ranch at night. When they returned, they discovered every head of beef cattle and the five horses which had been in the corral were gone, stolen by persons unknown. "Mister Strong, I thought you might be one of rustlers coming back for our little poke. Sorry if I seemed unfriendly."

Homer allowed he wished he had been home so he could have saved the herd.

Bart looked at the man and said, "No, Mister Jackson, no, you don't. If these are the men I believe them to be, you would have been killed, and your wife and daughters raped before they got around to killing them. Better you were gone."

The man had tears in his eyes and replied, "Mister Strong, those cows were all we had in the world. If we can't sell a beef cow or two along, we can't buy supplies or pay our bills."

Bart was somber and said, "Mister Jackson." Jackson interrupted Bart mid-sentence and asked to be called Homer.

Bart started again, "All right, Homer, the cows would help keep you alive, but you can always start over."

Homer went on to explain that they had five years invested in the piece of ground and had no intention of leaving it. Now that the cattle were gone, they had no way to make their mortgage payments.

While they had been talking, Jean, the younger of the two girls had opened the door and let the giant dog inside the cabin. She was holding onto the dog's neck and was rewarded with a big sloppy lick from the animal. She looked at Bart and asked, "What's your dog's name, Mister?"

Bart smiled at the little girl and said, "He ain't my dog, honey, but I call him Lucky."

"Whose dog is he?"

"He belongs to no one." And without the benefit of details, told the little girl he had found the dog on the trail.

The little girl turned to her father and said, "Can I keep Lucky, Papa? Please." Homer looked at Bart and was met with a shrug of the shoulders. He looked at Jean and said he would think on it.

Nellie May interrupted and said, "OK, fellas, let's put this conversation on hold for after dinner; I have beef stew and an apple pie which needs to be eaten." After days of eating bacon and beans, stew and apple pie sounded like manna from heaven to Bart.

After dinner, Homer and Bart sat at the table and enjoyed a nip of whiskey and smoked their pipes. After a long period of silence, Bart asked Homer, "How long have the cows been gone?"

"We came home just this afternoon to find them gone, so not more than a day."

Bart pondered a few moments and said, "I reckon I will get on their trail at first light. Maybe I will be able to catch up with your rustlers."

Homer looked at Bart and said, "I'm going with you, Mr. Strong."

"Homer, I am sure you're a hard worker and good father, but this ain't your line of work. If I find them, and if I come out of it alive, I will come back, get you, and you can bring your cows back home."

"Nope, they're my cows, and I'm going."

Bart looked at Homer and considered his options, perhaps the man could be of some help, if he would do exactly what he was told, but there was also the chance that the man would get himself killed. Bart said, "Homer, you will have to do exactly what I tell you to do. If you get yourself killed, your family will darn sure lose the farm and starve."

"OK. Mister Strong, you have my word."

The conversation was over, and Bart lay by the fireplace with his head on his saddle and got a good night's rest. At first light, he and Homer had coffee, visited the privy, and hit the trail in the direction of the tracks left by the cattle. As near as Bart could tell, there were four, maybe five, horses which were obviously carrying a load along with others that seemed to be without riders.

During the late afternoon of the second day, they heard the cattle bellowing and followed the sound. When they got fairly close, they dismounted, and Bart left Homer with the horses and dog and slowly walked towards the sounds of the cattle. Within a few yards, he came to the edge of an arroyo. The cattle were bunched about one-eighth of a mile away. Bart lay on the ledge and took out his binoculars and looked at the scene. There were dozens of longhorn cattle milling around and four men sitting at a campfire. Three or the four fit the description of the men he was looking for. The clincher was Jeff's black stallion with the white face, which was tethered to a tree.

Bart slid back and then stood up and went to Buck and took his Whitworth out of its scabbard. He checked the load and put in a new primer. He eased back to the ledge, laid down, took careful aim at the Indian who was facing him, centered the sight on his chest, and slowly squeezed the trigger. The impact of the .451 slug knocked the half-breed on his back. The other men jumped up, jerked out their revolvers, and started looking around. Bart slid back in order to hide his position and reloaded the Whitworth and eased back into position. The half-breed was clawing at the ground trying to pull himself towards the trees but making little progress. The other three men were hiding in the trees. As was so often the case during the war, this was to be a waiting game. Their water and rifles were by the campfire. Bart thought he might well get lucky, and one of the men would get careless and decide to get a canteen or rifle. Bart slid back again and walked to Homer and told him to start a small fire and brew a pot of Arbuckle. Homer looked at him quizzically but did as he was told. Bart took the saddle off Buck and the panniers off the packhorse and picketed them so they could graze. After getting the fire started, Homer followed Bart's lead and picketed his saddle horse.

Strong figured the three remaining men would stay behind the trees and try to sneak away under the cover of darkness. His only hope was that one of them would get careless and give him a clear shot before it got dark.

In a few minutes, Homer walked up fairly close and said, "Here is some hot coffee, Mr. Strong." Bart slid back out of sight, accepted the coffee, told Homer to stay by the fire, and then slid back into a shooting position. After about thirty minutes, Bart slid back and asked Homer to replace him and watch while he warmed his hands and feet. After a few minutes, they swapped places again. Right before dusk, Strong was rewarded for his patience. A large man with a big black mustache, who obviously thought he was well hidden, turned to get more comfortable and exposed the right side of his body. Bart was ready, and the man received a .451 slug through his thigh. The man screamed and wriggled back behind the tree. Unless the bullet had hit his thigh bone, the wound wouldn't kill him, but he would be leaking blood for a day or two and limping for a long time.

Bart slid back, went to the fire to warm himself, and reloaded the Whitworth. "Homer, go to the ledge and keep watch, just make sure you're not seen." A couple hours after dark, Bart heard the sounds of riders leaving the arroyo. He decided the high ground he commanded would be safest, so they stayed there all night. Bart and Homer took turns every thirty minutes or so sitting near the fire and warming hands and feet while the other man kept watch, hiding in the darkness wrapped in a blanket. Bart trusted Lucky to hear or see any intruders and warn them.

At first light, Bart went back to the ledge and surveyed the camp and trees with his binoculars and saw nothing beyond the half-breed slumped against a tree and Homer's cattle. Strong and Homer circled back about 200 yards and cautiously entered the arroyo. Bart figured the men were long gone, but kept constant watch for movement beyond the cattle milling around. The men were gone. Bart and Homer slowly walked their horses up to what had been the rustler's camp. They dismounted and walked to the place where the half-breed was laying and found a very dead and stiff carcass. Bart looked through the dead man's pockets and found a couple gold coins and a locket he had given Nettie on her sixteenth birthday. He wished he could kill the piece of crap again, slowly.

Bart walked to the panniers on his packhorse, took the leather folder out and wrote down "Cherokee Joe," the date, and signed the warrant. He put the gold coins in his pants pocket.

Even though he wasn't much help, Bart assisted Homer in rounding up the cows and together they drove the cattle back to the spread. Homer discovered that the giant dog was good with cattle and would be as much help to him as a playmate for Jean and Joan.

When they got the mustangs back in the corral, Bart said, "Well, Homer, you made some profit as it turns out. You got a sturdy looking saddle horse and rig out of this adventure."

Bart spent the night with the Jacksons and then said his goodbyes and wished Homer, Nellie May and the girls luck. He went to the corral and saddled Buck, put the panniers on the packhorse, and mounted.

Homer thanked him over and over for finding his cows and getting them back for him. Jean came running up with the dog and said, "Mister Strong, thanks for Lucky. I like that name, and he does too." Bart smiled at the little girl and was happy the dog would have a good home.

Bart shook hands with Homer and walked the horses out of the yard and towards Santa Fe. Three to go...

Chapter 15

After five days riding in light snow, freezing rain, and constant wind with some gusts up to thirty miles per hour, Bart arrived in Santa Fe, New Mexico, around mid-day. He had camped often, stayed in as many barns and outbuildings as possible to get out of the elements, and built several large campfires in order to warm himself when he couldn't find shelter. Still when he arrived in Santa Fe, he was nearly frozen to death. He found a livery and left Buck and the pack horse to be groomed and fed a scoop of oats. He then walked down the street carrying his Whitworth, Greener, and haversack to the La Fonda Hotel to find a room.

He stood in the lobby next to the stove, and the desk clerk brought him a cup of hot coffee and a blanket. After he warmed up a mite, he went to his room and left his Whitworth and haversack. He then came back to the lobby, thanked the desk clerk for his thoughtfulness and kindness, and asked directions to a barber shop and bath house. He decided to get the bath out of the way first so the barber wouldn't have to hold his nose while cutting his hair. He got some of the trail dust and grime beat off his clothes while he was in a hot tub of water soaking off the trail dirt and mud. Next stop was the barber shop where he got a shave and his hair trimmed. He didn't want to seem too obvious, so he asked if the barber had seen an old war friend of his which fit the description of Buryl Weathers. The barber contended he hadn't seen anyone who looked like the man Bart described.

Bart left the barber shop and went directly to the Missy Woods Café, laid the Greener in his lap, and had beef stew, cornbread, and a couple cups of coffee. He had gotten a good look at the three remaining men through his binoculars and knew he would recognize them on sight. One of the men wasn't part of the bunch he was after; that meant that one of the men had taken off on his own.

After eating, he walked across the street to the Pecos Saloon and took a chair at a table against the back wall, laid the Greener in his lap, and surveyed the room. He saw no familiar faces in the crowd. He had a beer and watched the room for about an hour. He got up and walked down the street to the Santa Fe Saloon and selected a table in the same general location in that room. Again, he ordered a beer, declined female company, and gazed at the faces in the room. No one resembled any of the three men he was hunting.

Bart wasn't really running low on money but saw no logic in running through his funds for no good reason and he needed something to occupy his mind while he waited out the winter. Some type job seemed the solution. He talked to the barkeep at the Santa Fe Saloon and asked him if he knew any business that might need help. He suggested Bart talk to the owner of the dry goods store. He walked over and introduced himself to the owner, Jedidiah Norwich, and asked him about the possibility of working in his store. As it turned out, Mr. Norwich was looking for someone dependable to fill in as his wife had been feeling poorly, and he had the place to himself. Bart thanked Norwich for the job and promised to see him the following morning at 8:00 AM sharp.

The wages they had agreed to wasn't much but would help pay for Bart's room, livery for his two horses, most of his eats at the Missy Woods Café, and relieve a lot of boredom. The men he was looking for obviously weren't in Santa Fe, and he had all he wanted of the trail until spring arrived and the weather moderated.

He worked an average of three days a week and whatever other hours requested by Mr. Norwich without complaint. Mrs. Norwich's health came and went. Sometimes Mr. Norwich had to spend more time with her than needed to run the store. Whenever Norwich needed Bart to cover the store, he showed up and did his best to satisfy the customers. When he wasn't working, he was in his room contemplating the killers of his family or reading month old newspapers, so work was a reprieve.

It was late in the afternoon on February 18, 1880, and the weather was blustery and cold, very cold. And like most days, the wind was making it worse. Bart had decided some time back that the men he was looking for weren't in Santa Fe. Mister Norwich wasn't keen on him wearing a sidearm in the store, so he left his gun belt, revolver, Greener, and Whitworth in his room at the hotel. While he was stocking the shelves behind the counter, he heard the door open, and when he turned to greet the customer, he was facing a young cowboy holding an old pearl handled Colt Paterson revolver in his hand.

"Hold on there. You don't need that shooter in here."

The obviously drunk young cowboy said, "Give me the money from the cash box, you ole coot."

"You don't want to do this, Son. Turn around and walk out of here."

"I'm not your son." With that the young cowboy shot Bart in the right side of his chest. The impact of the bullet knocked Bart against the shelves and cans tumbled down on and around him. The cowboy reached over the counter and took the money out of the cash box and ran out the door. He got about fifty feet before he was met by A. J. Foxx, the town marshal, who had been headed to the store, heard the gun shot, and started running. When the cowboy burst out of the door, Foxx cut him in half with a load of buckshot from a short-barrel shotgun. One man was wounded and another dead, and all over $33.00 and some change.

Luckily, the bullet that hit Bart was a .36 caliber and shot from an old black powder charge. The bullet embedded in tissue in Bart's upper chest but didn't hit any vital organs. There was a lot of bleeding, so the bullet must have nipped a vein. Bart lay on the floor wondering how he could go through a war, then years as a peace officer, and trail killers without a scratch and then get shot by some dumb drunken cowboy trying to steal money for whiskey and whores.

Carlos Gomez was the only sawbones in Santa Fe, and Marshal Foxx sent for him immediately. Three citizens lifted Bart up and took him across the street to the hotel and laid him on a large dining table.

Doctor Gomez arrived in about ten minutes and looked at the wound and said,

"That bullet has to come out." Doctor Gomez took Bart's belt loose, folded it twice, and told him to bite down on it so he wouldn't break his teeth when he started cutting and probing.

The doctor then requested lamps and people to hold them so he could see to probe for the bullet. Once the lights were in position, he motioned for the closest four men to hold Bart down, poured some whiskey over his knife and probe, then some in the bullet hole, took a healthy swig himself, and said, "Here we go, gringo. I think this is going to hurt." After the first cut and probe for the bullet, Bart lost consciousness.

When Strong woke up, he was bandaged and in a bed in a room he didn't recognize. In a few minutes, Mrs. Stella Goodson, a woman who came into the general store to buy linen and other fabrics every week and had chatted with him for a few minutes on each occasion, appeared. She came into the room with a pan of water and a small cloth. Mrs. Goodson dipped the cloth in the cool water and wrung it out somewhat then applied it to Bart's forehead.

Bart felt very hot, but he had his senses about him and said, "Mrs. Goodson, it ain't proper for you to be here in this room alone with me."

Mrs. Goodson smiled and replied, "I hardly think you are much of a threat to my rectitude right now, Mr. Strong. I'll worry about my virtue. You worry about getting well."

Stella took care of Bart for a little more than a week. After he was able to get up and around with a sling on his arm, Mrs. Goodson insisted he stay until he could fend for himself, but Bart was insistent he would be fine and moved back to the hotel. Jed Norwich had visited with Bart for a few minutes every day while he was confined to bed and filled him in on Stella Goodson during one of his visits.

Stella's husband had been a land speculator and had done well. He had managed to somehow shoot himself accidentally in the leg with a shotgun while turkey hunting in the spring of 1877 and died a couple weeks later after gangrene set in. They never had children, and Stella had never remarried. Although several men had courted her, none struck her fancy. Stella had turned the large home into a boarding house and made enough money between it and her sewing to make a comfortable living. Everyone in town agreed she was a fine woman. Bart would add: a very handsome looking woman to boot.

By the middle of March, Bart was fairly well recovered and, other than a little stiffness on his right side, felt little ill effects from the wound. He had tried to pay Stella for taking care of him and the room and board, but she steadfastly refused his money. However, when he invited her to dinner at the Missy Wood's Café, she smiled demurely and said she would like that very much. During the next couple months, Bart and Stella saw each other for lunch or dinner, either at the boarding house, where he insisted on paying for his meal, or the Missy Woods Café, most every day. Bart was sensitive about any hint of impropriety or indiscretion between him and Mrs. Goodson and was careful not to give any tongues something to wag about.

When they didn't eat in town, Bart and Stella took buggy rides, weather permitting, to the Santa Fe River and picnicked. Bart was attracted to Stella, and she seemed taken with him. On the 10th day of May 1880, Bart told Stella he had to leave. He hoped to return after he finished his business but had no idea how long he would be gone. He expected it would only be a matter of a few weeks or a couple months at most, but he couldn't promise. She told him she would still be around if she didn't get a better offer.

Early on the morning of May 11, 1880, Bart came by the boarding house with Buck and the pack horse and said goodbye to Stella. She cried a little, and he held her and told her he would be back. She handed Bart a sack full of corn dodgers and said, "If these were good enough for George Washington and Abraham Lincoln, they should keep you fortified for a few days on your trip." She turned and ran into the boarding house.

With a sack of Stella's corn dodgers, resolve, and a newfound sense of urgency, he headed out towards El Paso, Texas.

Chapter 16

Bart figured the trip to El Paso, Texas, would take about ten days. There were trading posts, stagecoach stops, watering holes, small ranches, missions, and the occasional small settlement along the route. Some of the settlements in New Mexico were so small they weren't even on the map.

As he rode along Bart was conflicted by his emotions. Was he betraying the memory of Mary Elizabeth by falling in love with Stella? He knew Mary would want him to be happy, but he still felt a twinge of guilt and uncertainty. He still missed Mary terribly and knew that she couldn't be replaced. Still, he had strong feeling for Stella and felt certain they could be happy together. Perhaps the fond memory of someone you loved wasn't meant to rob you of the opportunity for current happiness.

The killing was also taking a toll on his emotions. It was easy enough to kill a man who was trying to kill you or your family. It was quite another thing to take on the role of judge, jury, and executioner. Even if the crime deserved the punishment, the killing wore on you if you had an ounce of human compassion. Still, Bart had sworn to avenge the loss of his family and would see it through.

As he rode along deep in thought, the whiz and thud of an arrow brought him out of his reverie. The arrow was a mite low and hit the panniers on the pack horse. The arrow had come from Bart's left, no doubt from a clump of rocks around 100 yards away.

Bart rode Buck and led the pack horse into a stand of boulders, dismounted, and picketed both horses. He pulled the Whitworth from the scabbard and put a fresh cap on the nipple. There was an open space of a little more than 100 yards between the boulders he was using for cover and the rocks the Indians were hiding in. It would be an easy shot with the Whitworth, the problem was that there was nothing to shoot at.

Bart pulled his field glasses out of his saddlebags, eased to the side of the boulder, and scanned the rocks. There was no movement. He knew there were Indians, no doubt Apaches, hiding in the rocks just waiting for him to expose himself. As he scanned the area, he looked higher in the rocks and saw an Indian sitting cross-legged on a rock high above the rocks the Indians were hiding in. Counting the 100 yards across the span and the height, the solitary Indian was around 350 yards from Bart.

Bart was wrestling with what he should do. The Indian on the heights was probably the other Apaches' leader. Killing him might just get the rest of the Apaches to pull out. He hated to shoot a defenseless man, but the alternative wasn't all that appealing. Perhaps a compromise would work, he could just wound the Indian and if he didn't fall a couple hundred feet, it would send a message.

Bart adjusted the sight, engaged the set trigger, aimed, and squeezed the trigger. He watched and saw the bullet hit the Indian in the upper left arm. The impact of the bullet twisted the Indian around and he fell flat on the rock.

The Apaches in the rocks began boiling out like they were escaping a hornet's nest and started climbing the rocks towards the wounded man. Bart loosened the picket lines, mounted Buck, took the lead on the pack horse, and rode on down the trail as fast as the horses could run.

Fourteen days later, after escaping the Apaches, he still immersed in his soul searching, and he was still a good ways from El Paso. He had seen neither hide nor hair of the three men he was searching for. Strong didn't want to wear his horses or himself down, so he took his time. He stopped at least once each day or whenever he found people, whichever came first, and took a rest. At every place which had people, he inquired regarding the men he was hunting and always with the same result. No one admitted having seen the men.

Sometimes, he would receive an offer of a meal, and sometimes, the folks were just plain rude or unfriendly. More than once he was invited to spend the night in a barn and his horses given a scoop of grain. The people Bart encountered were mostly poor settlers and struggling to survive. He would always leave them some change to compensate for the grain for the horses or the food he ate. Most took the money with little if any protest.

Bart stopped at a small run-down looking farm outside the small village of Los Lunes, New Mexico. He walked his horses into the yard and hailed the house. A woman opened the door and asked if she could help him.

"I have been on the trail several days, and I was hoping I could do some chores in exchange for grain for my horses and perhaps a meal for myself."

"Mister, you've come to the right place. My name is Gabriella Smith, but folks hereabouts just call me Gabby. My husband's name is Nathaniel, we call him Nat. He got thrown off a horse he was trying to break last week, hit the corral fence, and busted some ribs. I could sure use some help if you could spare a couple days."

Bart realized right off why folks called the woman "Gabby." She didn't even seem to stop for a breath as she told him her circumstances.

As Bart looked around the spread, it was obvious Nat had been more than a little slack in the work department prior to getting thrown by the horse. There were a couple broken poles on the corral, perhaps from when Nat got thrown from the horse. Brush had grown up around the cabin. One door was loose and falling to one side on the barn. The garden had about as many weeds as vegetables, and the well rope was frayed and ready to break. There were other things badly in need of fixing, but Bart would have to take up residence in order to bring the entire spread into good repair. He had neither the time nor inclination for that task. Obviously, Nat was a slacker at best!

When Bart entered the cabin, he saw the inside was in about as much disarray as the outside. There was a man, he presumed Nat, lying on a bed and two boys who he would guess were around twelve or thirteen sitting by the fireplace. A girl he took to be about sixteen was working at the table kneading bread. Bart just shook his head, walked back out of the cabin, and led Buck and the pack horse to the barn. He took the saddle and panniers off the horses, and rubbed them both down with some straw. He found a crib containing grain and got each horse a scoop of oats.

Bart walked back to the cabin, stuck his head in the door, and said, "You boys come give me a hand." The boys, named Brett and Bruce didn't move a muscle and just ignored him. Bart looked at the two boys in amazement and said, "Boys, unless you're both deaf, you heard me, get off your backsides. I'm not accustomed to saying things twice. Let's get some of this work done."

The older boy named Brett turned and said, "And what if we don't, ole man?"

Bart looked at the boys in amazement and said, "Then I will teach you to respect your elders at the end of my belt, and then we will discuss what work needs to be done." Both boys looked at Bart with eyes wide open and considered their options. Something just told them this old man wasn't kidding, so they both got up and followed him towards the barn. Someone demanding they carry their weight on the farm was new to the boys, and they didn't quite know how to react. They had learned to do just what they must from watching their parents.

Bart decided to tackle the barn door first. Bruce found some nails and a hammer, and Strong got Brett to help hold the barn door in position. Bruce handed the nails to Strong one by one and helped hold the door while Bart nailed the rawhide hinge back in place. Bart asked them if there was a mattock on the place. They both look bewildered and finally, Brett asked, "What's a mattock?"

Bart described the tool. It was a pickax, with an adze and a chisel edge at the opposite ends of the head. Bruce said, "Oh, you mean a grubber!"

"Whatever you want to call it, get it." Strong put the boys to work digging out the brush alongside the cabin and pulling it away from the structure in a pile to burn. He went to the corral to see what could be done to repair the fencing. Bart spied a small grove of cedars about one-quarter mile from the cabin, walked over to the boys, and told them to take a break, get an axe, and follow him. Bruce produced an axe from the barn. When Bart looked at the axe, he found it to be dull and rusted. He supposed if one wasn't going to use tools there was no reason to keep them in good repair.

Bart asked the boys if there was a grinding wheel on the farm. Bruce took him to the back of the barn, and there, he found a dilapidated grinding wheel. Bart sharpened the axe as best he could.

"Let's go, boys." Bart walked towards the grove of saplings followed by the boys. He felled a couple of the trees and trimmed the branches off them. He looked at the boys and said, "Each of you grab one and drag it to the corral."

When they got back to the corral, Bart said, "I can handle this. Go finish digging out the brush." When Bart finished with the repairs on the corral fence, he walked over to the cabin and saw the boys had dug out about half the brush. Bart looked at the boys and said, "At the rate you two are working, the brush will grow back before you get done." Both boys bristled but went back at the task with renewed vigor.

About 5 PM, Gabby came to the door of the cabin and hollered, "Supper's ready." Neither of the boys had to be called twice and ran by Bart and through the door. When Bart got inside, the boys were going at the food, hammer and tongs, like they hadn't eaten in a week. He sat down at the table, took off his hat, and laid it crown down on a small stool near the table. He reached his plate over near the cook pot, spooned out some stew, picked up a slice of cornbread, and began to eat.

Both boys stopped and watched him with interest. Brett said, "Ole man, why do you eat so slow?"

"I don't eat nuthin that's gonna run away, so what's the rush?" Neither boy said anything, but Bart noticed they stopped gulping down their food and went at it with a more measured pace.

After finishing his supper, Bart took his plate and fork over and placed them next to the wash tub, picked up his hat, filled his coffee cup, and walked outside. He sat down on a large rock next to the door, built himself a smoke, and lit his pipe.

After a few minutes, the girl came outside and said, "My name is Millie, and I'm nearly sixteen." Bart said hello and continued with his smoke and sipped his coffee.

"Mister Strong, I hate it here. This place is falling down around us, and pa won't do much of anything but sit around and whittle." Bart looked at the girl and knew she was unhappy, and with good reason, but there wasn't anything he could do about her situation. He had tried to raise Nettie right and taught her responsibility, but this girl's problems were beyond his control.

Bart asked the girl if she had been born on the farm, and she explained they had only been in New Mexico for two years and her parents had bought the farm in good condition. Her father had written editorials for the Saint Louis Evening Post, and when it was bought out by the Saint Louis Dispatch, he lost his job. They had bought a Conestoga wagon and a couple plow horses, loaded some of their belongings, and headed west.

144

Millie was mature beyond her years and acknowledged that her father wasn't cut out for physical work and her mother wasn't much on housekeeping. Bart nodded slightly in agreement. Pushing a pen wasn't really strenuous and slackness became contagious.

The two boys came out of the cabin and sat down on the ground close to Bart and Millie. After sitting quietly for a few minutes, Bruce, the more outgoing of the two boys, looked at Bart and asked, "If we hadn't gotten up and come with you, what would you have done?"

Bart looked at Bruce and then his brother and said, "Boys, I never say anything I don't mean and can't back up. I would have taken off my leather belt and let you feel its bite until you decided to give me a hand."

Bart stayed on the small rundown spread for three days and repaired what was fixable. The boys joined in on the effort and seemed to enjoy the work. Their hands were bruised and blistered from weeding the garden and other tasks Strong pointed out to them, but they didn't complain.

When Strong had saddled Buck and gotten the pack horse ready, the boys came out of the cabin, shook his hand, and thanked him for helping them. Bart looked at the boys and told them that it appeared that their father was prone to be sickly and they were going to have to do a man's work, or the place would fall down around them.

They both grinned and Bruce said, "We kinda got that figured out the last couple days."

Bart walked Buck and the pack horse down the trail wondering if he had accomplished anything or if the boys would revert to their former ways and allow the place to fall back into disarray. Anyway, he had taught the boys something about responsibility and hoped they would measure up and take care of the place. Either way, El Paso was still a long ride.

Chapter 17

The western frontier was comprised of hard men. Life was harsh, demanding, and difficult. Most men were honest, hardworking, and as good as their word. Then there were the other kind who would rather steal than work and would cut your throat for a pocket watch or handful of change. Bart had learned from his war years it was always a good idea while on the trail in desolate country to be as mindful of what was behind you as you were of what was ahead. Many a time during the war, he had avoided capture by checking his back trail. Once he discovered men were trailing him, he took evasive action by hiding until they passed.

It had been two days since Bart had left the run-down Smith place. A couple hours after breaking camp and getting on the trail the third morning, Bart felt he was being followed. Men on the western frontier used all their senses: sight, sound, feel, smell, and taste; but the ones who lived the longest developed a sixth sense. Some called it intuition; others simply called it a gut feeling.

Beyond their five senses and feelings, western men learned to distinguish sounds. A human voice will echo no matter what it is trying to mimic. On the other hand, an owl or quail's call will never make an echo. A coyote or wolf might make a slight echo, but their sound is always easy to distinguish from the voice of a human trying to mimic the sound. It also benefited one to be wary and watch the actions of birds and small animals. When normal forest sounds stopped, it was time to grow cautious. Horses were also a dead giveaway to warn one of impending danger. If a horse swishes its tail, it is signaling some impending danger, and pricked ears indicate the same thing. Horses are prey animals, and their survival instincts are more sensitive to danger than humans. Thus, if their human companion is paying attention, the horse will alert a person to danger before it is humanly detectable.

For several hours, Bart had the uncomfortable feeling in his gut he was being followed. He had stopped and looked at his back trail several times through his binoculars and saw no riders, no dust, and no evidence of humans. Still he had a feeling of foreboding. Bart wasn't particularly good at tracking others, but he had an uncanny ability to sense when he was being tracked.

Just before sunset, Bart stopped and made camp in a small copse of fir trees. He removed the saddle from Buck and the panniers off the pack horse and picketed them so they could feed on the grass. He then got a small fire going and put on a pot of Arbuckle and got the skillet out to cook some bacon and a bite of beans. While the coffee was cooking, Bart considered the persistent feeling that he was being followed. He knew his fire could be seen for miles after dark. If there were people following him, they would see the flame, and come into the camp during the night to do their mischief. After eating, he leaned back, fixed a bowl of tobacco, smoked his pipe, and drank a couple cups of coffee. Bart was tired but really not sleepy. He lay with his head on the saddle, looked at the stars, thought about Stella, and wished this quest would soon be over.

According to his Elgin pocket watch, it was just after 10:00 PM. He knew that robbers or killers wouldn't come into the camp until they were certain he was asleep, so he figured he had a couple hours before he would have company. The night was warm, so he took his duster and extra blanket, rolled them up, and placed them on the ground in front of the saddle. He then took off his hat and placed it on the saddle and put the other blanket on the rolled up duster and extra blanket. He left his Whitworth leaning against a large fir tree next to the saddle and walked into the trees and darkness of the night. He sat down in front of a large tree, leaned back against it, checked the shells in his Greener, and laid his revolver on his lap.

Bart wasn't a particularly good shot with a pistol and only carried it to augment the Greener if worst came to worst. A .45 slug carried a punch, and he was good enough at close range to get the job done if needed.

Within an hour, his precautions were rewarded. The first sound he heard was a poorly mimicked quail call to his left and then an equally poor response from his right. Bart sat perfectly still and waited in the darkness. After a few minutes, he was rewarded by the sound of small twigs being broken as one of the men stepped through the trees towards his camp. Bart had chosen a spot about twenty-five feet from the camp fire but well-hidden against a tree and behind some small bushes. He stayed in his seated position and waited. In a couple minutes, two men appeared in the faint light of the campfire, one to his left and the other fairly straight ahead. The one on the left took aim and shot into the bedroll, and both men ran toward what they thought was Bart. At that point, Bart shot the larger of the two men who had shot into the bedroll. The load of buckshot from the Greener hit the man in the chest, blowing him off his feet, and flat of his back.

The other man dropped his rifle and said, "Mister, please don't shoot me. This was all Ollie's idea."

Bart slowly got up and said, "Don't turn around. Take that shooter out of the holster real easy with just your thumb and forefinger and let it drop on the ground and then turn really slow and let me see your face."

When the man turned to face Bart, he couldn't believe his luck. Before him stood none other than Wil Gabbage. Bart looked at Gabbage and said, "Sit down by the fire and put your hands atop your head and don't move." He then went over and picked up Gabbage's rifle and pistol, checked the man he had shot and found him very dead. A load of buckshot from a Greener at close range was quite lethal.

Bart took his hat off the saddle and flipped it to Gabbage and told him to throw him his hat. Bart looked at Gabbage and said, "Put on my hat, sit by the fire with your hands in your lap, and don't move. Try to get up and you will catch a load of buckshot" Gabbage didn't seem nervous, but Bart was cautious by nature. With that, Bart threw a couple sticks on the glowing coals, and within a minute, the flames renewed. Bart went back to his seat at the base of the tree and waited a little more than two hours. The only noise he heard was the occasional whippoorwill. Confident that only the two men were following him, Bart returned to the fire. Bart sat down across the fire from Gabbage, exchanged hats, and asked, "Do you know who I am?"

"No," replied Gabbage, "I have no idea."

"Does the name Bart Strong mean anything to you?"

Gabbage blanched white and started squirming, "Now just a minute. Let's talk about this."

"Gabbage, you talk, and I will listen. When I get tired of listening, I will let this Greener shut your mouth. Before you start, tell me where I can find James Smart and Buryl Weathers."

"Mister Strong, I don't have any idea where James Smart might be. He didn't state his intentions when we split up. After you killed Cherokee Joe when we rustled the cattle near Santa Rosa, Weathers told us he was going to El Paso. We parted company and I haven't seen him since." Bart looked at the man and was amazed at how weak of courage he was. Bart had the distinct feeling that Gabbage was lying to him, but about what, he had no idea.

Bart said, "You and your friends killed my daughter and my grandchildren. Four of you are dead, and that number is going to change to five by daylight."

Gabbage was whimpering and said, "My God, Strong, I have never killed anyone in my life. I swear." With that, he lost his water.

Strong acknowledged to himself that the man probably didn't have the courage to kill a rabbit. Nonetheless, Gabbage had raped his daughter and did nothing to stop the killings. Bart knew Gabbage wouldn't have had the courage to stand up to the Weathers gang, but he participated in the shameful act. With that thought in his mind, Strong shot Gabbage in the chest with a load of buckshot from the Greener.

Bart felt little satisfaction as he sat by the fire drinking coffee and contemplated the enormity of his actions until first light. He sat back from the light of the fire and wondered when and how this would end. Strong remembered an axiom he had read, "Revenge is a dish best served cold." As time went on, his embitterment towards the killers of his daughter and her family increased. He was beginning to feel a measure of satisfaction by killing the men and didn't like the change in himself he was experiencing.

He went into the trees and retrieved the two horses belonging to the dead men, took their saddles off, and set them free. With some effort, he dragged the two bodies together and checked their pockets. He found about $50.00 between the two men. He figured they wouldn't need the money where they were going and put the cash in his pocket. He didn't see anything among their weapons or gear he needed, so he threw the weapons and saddlebags on their bodies and placed their saddles near their carcasses.

The man Gabbage had referred to as Ollie was the man Bart had seen at the campsite before he shot the Indian, or half-breed as it were. Weathers was the man he had put the bullet from the Whitworth in his thigh.

Strong took the leather folder from his haversack, pulled out a form, wrote the date and "Will Gabbage" on it, signed, and returned the form to the folder. He then loaded the panniers on the pack horse, stowed the coffee pot and skillet, saddled Buck, put the rawhide loop holding the Greener on the saddle pommel, and placed the Whitworth in its scabbard. Bart swung into the saddle and walked the horses through the trees without the slightest glance back. Two to go…

Chapter 18

Weathers and Smart were the worst of the seven, or at least the most lethal with a gun. If Bart wanted to survive his self-appointed mission, he would have to be very, very careful and give them no opportunity.

Bart had been riding for about four hours and decided it was time to take a break and have a cup of coffee. He selected an outcrop of large boulders to help cut the wind and stopped in a small clearing between large rocks to avoid the wind. Just as he swung down from the saddle, a bullet whizzed by his head. He scurried behind one of the boulders and waited to see what was going to happen next. Bart felt naked. The Greener and Whitworth were both on Buck. At further than ten to fifteen feet, his S & W .45 was about as useful as a boat anchor in the desert.

The problem was, Bart didn't know where the shot had come from, fairly near or far, and he wasn't completely sure of the direction. It was extremely difficult to gauge the direction of a single shot because of the reverberation of the sound. As the sound bounces around it makes it almost impossible to pinpoint the origin. Bart had used this knowledge during the war to mask his location. Hit or miss, he only shot once. Bart felt certain the shot had come from a higher elevation because the boulders would have made a flat shot impossible unless the shooter was very close. If the shooter had been close, he probably wouldn't have missed! It was only the ego of the assassin that saved Bart's life. Only an idiot would try for a head shot from any appreciable distance. The trunk of the human body provided the largest target and the greatest possibility of a kill shot.

Strong had been shot at many times during the Civil War, mostly just wild shooting in his general direction after he had shot some officer or artillery soldier. The key was to get on his horse and get away from the area before the soldiers could get a search party organized and send it to look for him. The circumstances here were different. He was the one being shot at from cover. He didn't like the shoe being on the other foot.

Bart wriggled around to the side of the boulder and peeped up at the foothills. There was plenty of cover to hide the shooter. He saw no horse. Had the shooter left thinking he had hit Bart? Or was the horse picketed out of sight and the man still hiding? Most likely, the shooter was just waiting for him to make a mistake and come into the open so he could try another shot. Bart cursed himself for not realizing a third man was following him, but it was too late now. He had figured, wrongly, that if there were others with the two men who came into his camp, they would have revealed themselves after two hours. No one did. Obviously, Gabbage was more afraid of the third rider than he was of Strong because he gave no hint of a third man.

Bart called Buck. The horse came over close enough he could grab the reins, and the horse joined him behind the boulder. Strong got the Whitworth, checked the load, and put in a new primer. He took his binoculars out of the haversack and peered around the boulder with the glasses. Game on. After looking for a couple seconds, he would pull his head back behind the boulder, wait a minute or two, and then peek again for a couple seconds. After several minutes of this maneuver, Bart saw a glint of reflected sunlight for just a split second, and then it was gone. Bart reckoned the distance to be about 300 yards and 200 feet higher in elevation. He adjusted the Soule sight on the Whitworth, took aim, and fired at the point at which he had seen the reflection. He was rewarded by a scream and loud cursing from whoever was up there.

Bart figured the man wasn't seriously hurt. The bullet had probably caused rock fragments to fly and hit the man. He would be hurting but probably not incapacitated.

Now, it was a waiting game to see who flinched first. If the man tried to sneak away during the afternoon, Bart would have the advantage and nail his hide to the wall, so he figured the man would probably wait for darkness. On the other hand, Bart couldn't leave his position either without giving the dry gulcher a shot at him. About an hour after dark, Bart heard the sound of rocks tumbling down the hillside and figured the man was making his exit. He took the saddle off Buck and the panniers off the pack horse and picketed them.

Strong made a small fire and boiled some coffee and depended on his horses to alert him if anyone approached. He was careful to stay out of the light of the campfire and waited out the night while taking a catnap from time to time. The next morning, Bart saddled Buck and walked him slowly up towards the point where he had seen the reflection and aimed his shot. When he got close, he dismounted and walked along slowly with his Greener cocked. In a few yards he found several cigarette butts, a spent .44 shell, and a fair amount of blood. Maybe he had hit the man after all. The boot prints indicated the man who had tried to dry gulch him was large, or at least had big feet. Bart followed the boot prints and found where the shooter's horse had been picketed. The man

158

had tied his mount around a bend in the terrain where it couldn't be seen from Bart's location.

Confident the man was long gone, Bart went back to his camp, cooked some breakfast, and thought on what had happened. Obviously, either Weathers or Smart had tried to dry gulch him. From what little he had been told, Smart fancied himself a gunfighter so he would probably have come at him straight on and up close. Weathers on the other hand would be more cautious and apt to lay in wait. If it was Weathers, and everything indicated it was, he had some hard bark on him, he got a .451 slug through his thigh and now an injury that brought plenty of blood, and he was still kicking.

Whoever it was, could read sign and knew when he heard the two distinctive shotgun blasts more than an hour apart that Strong had killed both men who had been sent into the camp the night before. Realizing the two men had failed, the dry gulcher decided he would take care of Strong himself. Only because Strong was leaving the saddle at the same instant as the shot had he failed.

Bart saddled Buck, loaded the panniers on the pack horse, and continued on his trip, now more cautious than ever as he was becoming the hunted as well as the hunter. Now that the man had been unsuccessful in dry gulching Bart, he would be more selective and find a closer spot next time.

Bart knew his limitations and saw no logic in trying to track the bushwhacker through the rough terrain. That could get him killed if the man laid in wait for him to come along.

Bart reckoned it was certainly taking him a long time to get to El Paso, and after this last encounter, he would be traveling even slower and more cautiously for the rest of the trip.

Chapter 19

On a whim, Bart decided to go to San Lorenzo Canyon, outside Polvadera, in Socorro County, New Mexico. It was possible that the man who had taken a shot at him might just have decided to hole up there and allow his new wound to heal. Wade Russell had told Bart about San Lorenzo County when they were discussing possible hideouts Strong might want to consider checking while going after the killers.

After he had ridden a few miles into the canyon, he saw some rock and adobe shacks. Everything was covered with a layer of dust. *Polvadera* meant dust in Spanish. He stopped in front of a small run-down building which had a hand painted sign displaying "Salun." He hitched Buck and the pack horse to the rail, took out his Whitworth and Greener, and went into the nasty looking watering hole. The bar was unkempt, covered with dust, tobacco juice leavings were all around the spittoon, and there were only three customers. There were two dirty looking men at one table and a young kid at another.

Bart sat down at a table at the back of the room and leaned the Whitworth against the wall beside his chair. He placed the Greener in his lap, ordered a beer, and asked if the place had food. The barkeep said they had beans, so Bart reluctantly ordered a plate to go with the beer.

Neither of the grubby looking men looked anything like either of the men he was trailing. The young kid who was sitting by himself was interesting. The boy was very short and slight of build with blue eyes that were in constant motion. There was something about the kid that made the hackles on the back of Bart's neck stand up.

The barkeep brought Bart a plate of hot beans flavored with chilies and a hard piece of cornbread, and he began to eat. These were spicy Mexican beans, and Bart knew they were going to play havoc with his innards, but he had to admit they were tasty. After a few bites, the kid said, "Ole man, what are you doing here?"

Bart continued to slowly eat his beans, took a nibble of the cornbread, looked at the kid for a few moments, smiled, and said, "Eating beans." He then reached his right hand down under the table and cocked the hammer on the right barrel of the Greener which was lying in his lap.

The kid stared at Bart like he couldn't believe this old coot was sassing him, but he heard the obvious click of the hammer and became cautious. The two men sitting at the other table started getting interested in the conversation and were wondering how this was going to play out.

"Ole man, I asked you what you are doing here?"

Bart continued eating until he finished the beans, slid the plate across the table, leaned back in his chair, looked at the kid, and replied, "I was eating beans. Now I'm drinking my beer."

The kid slapped his hand on his table and immediately wanted to know if Bart knew who he was. Bart looked the boy over and said, "I don't know, just some woman's son I guess. I have absolutely no idea who you are and don't really care."

The kid sat up straighter in his chair as tall as he could and said, "William Bonney, but most people call me Billy the Kid."

Bart looked at the boy for a couple seconds, smiled, and said, "Makes sense to me. Billy is a version of William, and you are a kid."

The kid hit the table again, this time with his fist, and said, "Are you making sport of me?" Bart took the Greener by the pistol grip, cocked the left hammer, and laid the shotgun on the table loosely pointing in the direction of the kid. He then smiled at the kid and said, "Whatever I'm doing here has nothing to do with you. I never heard of you, and I have no business with you."

The kid allowed that no one would come to the filthy camp in San Lorenzo Canyon unless they were tracking someone. Bart just shrugged his shoulders and made no reply. The kid was getting more fidgety and angry by the second, and Bart figured he had better defuse the situation before it got out of hand and he had to kill the boy. "Son, you're right. I'm tracking someone, but it ain't you and has nothing to do with you."

"I've killed several men, and there is a big reward to bring me in dead or alive. A lot of people are looking for me."

Bart looked at the kid and finally answered, "I'm sure you are a bad man, but I'm not a bounty hunter and have no interest in you one way or the other." Bart looked the kid straight in the eyes and said, "This Greener has both barrels pointed right at you. I've also killed several men and I could have killed you any time since I sat down. I'll tell you this only one last time. I've no interest in you, what you have done, or who is looking for you."

The kid looked at Bart for a full minute as he processed what the old man had said and then responded, "Yeah, I guess you could have killed me. Alright, sorry I got on my high horse." Bart told him it wasn't a problem, paid for the beer and beans, and walked out of the dump, keeping the kid in his line of sight until he got out of the door.

****

On the morning of April 1, 1878, Sheriff William Brady was walking down the main street in Lincoln, New Mexico, when William Bonney shot him several times from hiding. Bonney was captured and convicted of the murder of Sheriff Brady but broke out of jail and killed a jailer while making his escape. Bonney was killed by Pat Garrett on July 14, 1881, at Fort Sumner, New Mexico. Henry McCarthy, aka William Bonney, aka Billy the Kid, is thought to have killed a dozen or so men during a five-year period. He was not yet twenty-two years old when he was killed.

Pat Garrett was killed beside a road outside Las Cruces, New Mexico, on February 29, 1908, when he stopped and got off his horse to take a leak. He was shot in the back of the head with a rifle. A goat rancher named Wayne Brazel, who Garrett had tried to evict from his spread, was charged with the assassination. Brazel was acquitted, and no one was ever convicted of the murder of Garrett. He was fifty-seven years old at the time of his death.

****

Bart had suspected who the kid was when he first saw him because a kid was rarely seen by himself in the west. Bonney confirmed his suspicion. Bart wasn't about to give the little twerp the benefit of acknowledging that he had heard of the notoriety of the killer. Confident he was wasting his time in this dust infested place, Bart mounted Buck, took the lead of the pack horse, and went back out of the canyon toward Socorro, New Mexico.

Chapter 20

Bart rode for two days resting frequently and, as evening approached stopped and made camp for the night. Even though the nights were still chilly, Bart decided, based entirely on instinct, not to build a fire and spent the nights in cold camps. The feeling he wasn't alone was back with him, and he had learned not to ignore his gut instinct. He was up at daylight and started to build a fire when he heard the sound of gunfire which seemed to be coming from the west and less than a mile away. Bart quickly saddled Buck and put the panniers on the pack horse and set out in the direction of the shooting.

As he got closer to the sound of firearms, he grew cautious, dismounted, and tied the horses to a tree. He took out the Whitworth, checked the load, put in a new primer, and eased through the copse of trees toward the shooting. When he came to the edge of the tree line, he was overlooking a small valley which contained a cabin, corral, and a couple of small outbuildings.

Bart looked the situation over with his binoculars and saw there were two ox carts and at least five Comancheros hiding behind the carts firing at the cabin.

****

Comancheros had transitioned from traders of pots and pans and other household utensils to running guns and whiskey to the Indians. Of late, they had discovered a more lucrative revenue source. They had taken to stealing horses and taking prisoners, preferably young girls, to sell in Mexico or ransom back to the relatives of the hostages. Comancheros were a mixed breed of Pueblos, Comanches, Apaches, Kiowas, and Navajos, often inbred with Mexicans. There were often Anglos mixed in as well. Comancheros were a bad lot and infested both Texas and New Mexico.

****

Bart leaned the Whitworth against a tree and sighted in on a large man who was nearest him, a relatively easy target at a little less than 600 yards. Bart engaged the set trigger, took a deep breath, and gently squeezed the trigger, and the heavy rifle bucked against his shoulder. A second later, the large man landed on his butt, sat with a puzzled look on his face, and began twitching in death throes. Bart eased back in the trees and reloaded the rifle, put in a new primer, and went back to the same tree. The

168

Comancheros had stopped firing at the cabin and were trying to figure out where the shot which had killed their companion had come from.

The Comancheros were now caught in a crossfire. When one of them shifted to get behind the end of the cart to shield himself from Bart's location, a shot from the cabin caught him in the shoulder. As he was wriggling back to the side nearest Strong, Bart carefully sighted and shot another man in the thigh. The two remaining healthy Comancheros loaded the dead man and the two wounded individuals on the carts and started the oxen away from the cabin while trying to keep the carts between themselves and the two shooters.

Bart took no pleasure in needless killing, and the Comancheros had realized they were whipped and were pulling out. There was no need to kill them now as they were no longer a threat. Bart waited until the Comancheros were out of sight and then went back to the horses and mounted Buck, took the lead of the pack horse, and started towards the cabin, riding very slowly and making sure his hands were visible.

When Bart entered the yard, a young man came out the door and greeted him, "Thank goodness you came along when you did. What in the world did you shoot those men with? They had to be at least 600 yards away from you."

Bart looked at the man for a moment and said, "Yep, about 600 yards, and it is a .451 caliber Whitworth rifle."

"Well you and that special rifle sure saved our bacon. I'm Elmer Jensen. Won't you come into the cabin and meet my family and have some coffee."

Bart hitched Buck and the pack horse to the porch, loosened their cinches, and entered the cabin. Once inside, Elmer introduced Strong to his wife Joanne and the kids, a boy of about twelve named Paul and a younger girl named Katherine, who they called Kate. Joanne produced two cups and poured both men a cup of hot strong coffee and then disappeared, taking the kids to the back of the cabin behind a sheet hanging from the ceiling.

After sampling the coffee, Bart filled his pipe, lit it, and leaned back in his chair. "This is a nice place you have here. Good grass and a stream."

Elmer thought for a minute and responded, "This is Valencia County which is situated in part of the Rio Grande Valley. The grass is plentiful most of the time, but since the soil is too poor for farming, we raise a few head of Longhorn cattle, tend a garden, and try to make ends meet."

Bart looked at Elmer and replied, "Well it looks like you are doing well. Everyone seems happy and well fed."

"We are just hanging on" replied Elmer. "We get what few necessities we must have from the trading post in Los Pinos or Belen. The problem is, the Indians come off the reservation and steal our steers, and now the Comancheros come by trying to steal our horses and children. There are cattle all over these hills, but I can't gather them alone. And it will be some time before Paul is old enough to help."

Strong was thoughtful for a few moments and then said, "Mr. Jensen, it is none of my business what you do or how you raise your children, but out here, if a boy can sit a horse, he can help. We had boys Paul's age wearing uniforms and playing drums during the war. I just met a man a short while back who has been on his own since he was eleven. Bart gave Jensen a few moments to chew on what he had said and continued, "Mr. Jensen, I'm not on a fixed timetable and can hang around a few days and see if we can discourage some of these cattle rustlers, if you like"

"Mr. Strong, please call me Elmer. You don't know how much I appreciate your offer, but I can't ask you to take on my problems."

"Elmer, I don't recall you asking. You folks remind me of my family which I lost. An old friend helped them get started, and maybe I now have an opportunity to repay his kindness by helping you."

Elmer expressed his condolences regarding the loss of Bart's family, told him he could put his gear in the shed, put his horses into the corral, and give them a scoop of oats. Elmer said, "We can start scouting around tomorrow morning if you want."

Bart and Elmer were up early, had coffee, saddled their horses, and headed out. The first and second days were uneventful, and they returned to the spread for supper and a night's rest. Around noon on the third day, Bart spotted three men with his binoculars leading two cows into a narrow arroyo. Bart turned to Elmer and said, "They're your cows. How do you want to handle this?"

Elmer looked at Bart and slowly shook his head and replied, "I don't hold with killing, but if this doesn't stop I will be burying my children from starvation. Let's do what we have to do."

Bart told Elmer to stay back from the edge so he wouldn't be noticed, ride down to the end of the arroyo, and wait until he heard a rifle shot. That would be the signal that at least two Indians were headed his way. Bart told him he would give him time to get settled before he fired on the Indians. Bart dismounted, waited about ten minutes, moved up a couple hundred yards, laid the Whitworth across the saddle, put an Indian in his sights, and slowly squeezed the trigger. The Indian he had selected was jerked out of the saddle, and the other two lit out, leaving the wounded man and the cows. Bart mounted Buck and worked his way carefully into the arroyo and went up to the man on the ground. He had hit the man exactly where he wanted. Unfortunately, for the man, the bullet deflected off a shoulder bone and went through a lung. Bart got off Buck and walked to the man and saw he was near death. Frothy blood was coming from his mouth and he was gasping for air. Bart looked at the man and said, "I wasn't trying to kill you, but stealing cattle can be a fatal occupation."

About that time, Bart heard two rifle shots in rapid succession. He mounted Buck and rode down the arroyo. When he rounded a corner, he came upon two Indians who were on the ground. One was dead, and the other had a bullet hole in his thigh. It appeared the .44 slug had missed the bone and left a sizable exit hole. It looked as if the man would live.

Bart cut the shirt off the dead Indian, wrapped the leg of the live man, and helped him onto his horse. Bart looked at the man and said, "Tell your friends there is nothing but death waiting for them if they come here to steal more cattle. We will turn the horses loose, and you can come back to get your dead. Just don't come back for anything else."

Bart and Elmer herded the two cows back toward the cabin in silence. Once they had gotten the saddles off their mounts, Elmer spoke up, "Mr. Strong, that was the first human I ever killed. I feel sick about it."

Bart looked at him and said, "Son, if you ever get to the point you enjoy killing another human being, you better take inventory of yourself. Sometimes in a land of few laws and even fewer lawmen to enforce them, killing can be a necessity but not something which should be enjoyed."

Bart reflected on the number of men he had killed thus far on his quest. He was sure some of the men he shot during the Civil War had died, but that hadn't been his goal. Since he left Bolivar, Missouri, he had killed several men, and not all were involved in any way with the murder of his family. He was uneasy with the way killing could become easier as the bodies stacked up. He was afraid he was beginning to become hardened to the point human life was losing its value.

Bart spent the night with the Jensens. After an early morning cup of coffee and a stack of flapjacks, he was on the trail again, on his way to Socorro, New Mexico. He had no idea if Elmer would teach Paul how to use a firearm or get him involved in the work on the ranch. That was his business.

Bart took no pleasure in killing the Indian, but since the west was an unforgiving place, sometimes equally cold-hearted responses were the only solution to lawlessness. In this case, the Indians could have been content with eating reservation food and left the Jensen cattle alone; rather, they chose to steal the cows. Elmer Jensen could have ignored the cattle being stolen and allowed his family to starve; not much of a decision involved there. He was happy he could help the young couple, and he hoped they would survive and prosper. This was a harsh and unforgiving land. Jensen would have to grow some hard bark for he and his family to survive.

Bart had done what he could. It was up to Jensen now.

Chapter 21

Bart was going to go through Socorro, New Mexico, in a few days, so he decided to write a letter to Stella and tell her how things were going and post it as he passed through the town.

Dear Stella,   *August 3, 1880*

I'm not much of a letter writer but wanted to tell you I am well and nearing the end of my mission. Perhaps with luck, I will be back in Santa Fe before spring. It is miserably hot here and I seldom experience a breeze.

I miss you terribly. After years of loneliness and then bitterness you have brought a measure of contentment and joy to my heart. The corn dodgers weren't bad either.

I doubt you have any long-term interest in an ole coot like me, but I intend to propose marriage to you when I return. This letter will give you time to think on that.

Yours,

Bart

Strong addressed the envelope and put it in his wallet. Four days later, he was in Socorro, New Mexico, and posted the letter. He was told the stagecoach would take the letter in a few days, and the addressee should have the letter within a week or so, barring bad weather or mishaps. Content the letter would find its way to Stella, Bart walked over to the barber shop and got a shave and hair trim then used the tub in the back to get the first few layers of trail dust and grime off his body. A Mexican girl took his clothes out back and beat them with a wire whip to get most the dust and dirt off them and brought them back to Strong.

When Bart came out of the barber shop, he looked across the street and saw the Cactus Saloon and Eatery and thought, "*why not.*" He went into the establishment and ordered a beer, beef steak, fried taters, apple pie, and of course, a pot of coffee to rinse down the pie. While Bart was eating, he overheard some cowboys at a nearby table talking about some gunfighter who had joined their drover crew for a trail drive going to Tucson, Arizona. Strong leaned back in his chair and said loud enough to be heard by the cowboys, "Excuse me, I couldn't help but overhear your conversation about the gunfighter. What does this gunfighter look like?"

The older man of the three looked Strong over and said, "What's your interest in this man, Mister?"

Bart smiled a disarming grin and replied, "Well, perhaps nothing until I know what he looks like."

The man considered the response for a few seconds and said, "He is tall, has brown hair, shaves each day, keeps his hair combed, wears two Colt Peacemakers in cross-draw fashion, and is a pain in the arse. Sound like somebody you might know?"

"No, and under normal circumstances doesn't even sound like someone I would want to know, but I need to see him about a personal matter."

"Well, we are camped four to five miles to the west outside Socorro and will be leaving at first light the day after tomorrow. If you want to see him, it needs to be today or tomorrow."

Bart thanked the man for his help, got up, tipped his hat, and walked toward the batwing doors of the saloon. As he got near the doors, Bart turned and walked back to the cowboys and asked, "One more thing: is the owner of the cattle with the herd, or do I need to see a trail boss?"

The same cowboy with whom he had been conversing said, "Captain Swint is the owner, and he is with the herd."

Bart looked at the man and asked, "Is this Swint fellow old, grumpy, and with a missing index finger on his right hand?"

"Yes, he does have a missing finger. But he pays me, so I'm not going to comment on him being grumpy. Do you know him?"

Bart chuckled and said, "It's been awhile, but yes, I know him." After the comment, Bart walked out of the saloon.

Bart took the pack horse to the livery, took off the panniers, and asked the hostler to wipe him down and give him a scoop of oats. He told the man he would be back in a couple hours to stable the saddle horse. With that, Bart started Buck out at a trot towards the camp he had been told about. After about thirty minutes, Strong spied the camp and walked his horse in close to the campfire and chuck wagon. John Swint was sitting on a small folding chair, drinking a cup of coffee, and looking as grumpy as he had fifteen years prior. Bart stayed on Buck and said, "Most well-mannered men would ask a man to get down off his horse for a cup of coffee."

Swint swung around and replied, "Who the hell said I was... Well, I'll be damned. Bart Strong. Marcus told me some ole coot might be coming to see me. How long has it been?"

Bart said, "You're just as charming as ever, I see. It's been a while. Can I get off my horse now?"

Strong and Swint spent the better part of an hour reminiscing about the war and catching up on what each had been doing. Swint had been the top sergeant of the scouts' detachment when Bart was serving with General Nathan Bedford Forrest in his Tennessee campaigns, and they had gotten along well. After the war, General Forrest had become the first Grand Wizard of the Ku Klux Klan but left the organization in 1869 and ordered it disbanded. It wasn't.

Bart filled John in on what had happened to his family and tied the murders to John Smart. Swint said Smart was with them, but he was short-handed of drovers even with him. Swint said, "I sympathize with your circumstance, but if you kill him, you've got to fill in until we get this herd to the railhead in Tucson, Arizona. Bart, if I lose this herd, I lose my ranch."

Bart looked John in the eye and said, "John, all I know about cattle is they make a good beef steak. I don't know how I could help you."

"I tell you what, Bart. If you live through the encounter with Smart, which ain't a given, you can replace my scout. He's a good trail hand, and I can bring him in to work the herd, Deal?" Bart agreed, and Swint said "Smart is with some of the other drovers in town right now. He will be riding the early morning shift and will be in the camp shortly after daylight tomorrow morning, if that's of interest to you."

"I'll be here, and if I'm alive, I'll scout for you to Tucson."

Bart spent the night sleeping fitfully and was up around 4 AM, got his horses from the livery, and trotted them to the cattle camp. After loosening the horses' cinches and picketing them, he removed the Greener from the saddle pommel, got a cup of coffee, and sat on the ground with his back against a Narrowleaf Cottonwood tree. He cocked both barrels of his Greener and laid it on his lap. Smart and one other man rode up to the camp at first light and got a cup of coffee and a plate of beans. As Smart walked up to within about fifteen feet in front of him, Bart put his hand on the pistol grip and pointed the Greener at Smart and called out, "James Smart, I'm here to serve an execution order on you."

"You're crazy. I ain't never been in no court and convicted of murder."

"You were tried in 1879 in absentia along with five others for the murders of Jeff Spencer, his wife and children, and Juan Gonzalez, a Mexican. I'm here to serve the order." Cowboys who had been eating started gathering up their cups and plates and getting out of the way.

Captain Swint spoke up and said, "All you boys get on your horses and go to the herd, so they won't stampede when the fireworks start." It was all arses and elbows as the cowboys dumped their cups and plates in the wash pot, sprinted to their horses, and exited the camp. Swint just sat on his stool and sipped his coffee.

Smart poured his coffee on the ground, flipped the cup towards the chuck wagon, and said, "You don't give me much of a chance with that scattergun pointed at my innards."

"Well, Smart, I didn't come here to give you a chance. I came to kill you plain and simple. I just wanted you to know the reason you are about to die. Get prepared to join your friends in hell." The gunfighter dropped the plate of beans, and suddenly, the force of the double loads of buckshot lifted Smart off his feet and flung him on his back onto the campfire. Strong mumbled to himself, "You had a better chance than you gave Jeff, Nettie, and the kids."

Swint said, "Darn, Bart, help me get him out of the fire so he doesn't stink up the camp." They each took hold of a boot and together dragged the carcass out of the fire. After the shots, the drovers began coming back into the camp and dismounted. When they were fairly well assembled around the camp fire, Bart said, "The black stallion with the white face is named Blackie and was my son-in-law's favorite horse. I will ride him some on the trail and then take him back home with me. Everything else belonging to Mr. Smart is there for the taking."

The cattle punchers relieved the body of the fancy gun belts and pistols and the Spencer from Smart's horse. A drover with a worn out saddle took the saddle off Smart's horse and exchanged it with his. Swint went to the body and took about $75.00 out of Smart's pockets and gave the money to Cookie for safekeeping. The funds would be used as bar money for Tucson.

While the group of drovers were in the camp, Swint explained why Strong had killed James Smart. About midway through his explanation, a tall string bean cowboy interrupted and said, "Boss, he's been bulldozing all of us since he joined up. We figured he would get the wrong pig by the tail sooner or later!" To a man, they found no fault with Bart and were glad to have him with the outfit.

Swint explained what Bart's function had been during the war and allowed he would be more than adequate to scout ahead of the herd.

Strong got up and walked over to his haversack, took out a leather bound binder, and removed a sheet of paper on which he recorded the date, "John Smart," signed the form, and placed it back with the other five.

Bart got a cup of coffee and sat by himself thinking about Nettie and the grandchildren he had never met. One to go...

Chapter 22

Bart took his Whitworth and scabbard off Buck and the panniers off the pack horse and gave them to Cookie for safekeeping in the chuck wagon. He handed the Greener to the cook, smiled, and said, "That thing will hurt you, be careful." He placed the horses with the remuda. He turned to Swint and asked if he had a Winchester he could borrow while scouting in front of the herd. Swint walked over to the chuck wagon and took out a blanket in which was wrapped one of the new Winchester Model 1876 Centennial rifles which was chambered in the .45-75 caliber. The new rifle had been unveiled at the World's Fair in Philadelphia, Pennsylvania, in May 1876. John explained that he had won the weapon from a cattle buyer in a card game in 1878. He doubted it had ever been fired. Swint handed it to Bart and walked back to the wagon, unlocked the cartridge crate, and got him two boxes of shells for the rifle. He looked at Strong and said, "Why don't you take the scabbard that was on Smart's saddle? None of the drovers need it, and I don't think Smart is going to be using it."

Bart spent the rest of the day discussing the drive with Swint, and talking to the different drovers, trail drive cook, and

185

remuda manager, and in general, getting to know most of the hands. In private talks none of the men blamed him for killing Smart, who had bulldozed some of the men and tried to goad them into a fight, probably to scare them into pulling his turn riding drag or take his turn relieving the bobtail guard.

The West of the mid and late 1800s was filled with hard men who would overlook or forgive many things for the greater good. The exception was that harming or killing a woman or child was universally condemned on the frontier even by the most ruthless characters. A man might steal or cheat at cards, but there were two absolutes on the frontier: keep your word and respect women and children. Anyone who violated either of those unwritten rules deserved what he got, so none of the wranglers faulted Strong for taking the killer's life. Bart spent one of the more tranquil nights he had enjoyed in some time in the cattle drive camp.

At first light, Bart got a cup of coffee and a plate of oatmeal with some sorghum spooned on top. After eating and having a second cup of coffee, Bart saddled Buck, told Swint he would be back by nightfall, walked the horse out of the camp, and then put him into a ground eating canter towards the west. It was about 200 miles from Socorro, New Mexico, to Tucson, Arizona, as the crow flies. The problem was cattle couldn't sprout wings and fly across a mountain, and the Gila Mountains stood in the way of cutting straight across to Arizona. The Gila comprised about three million acres of heavily forested mountains, gorges, and meadows which would be turned into a national forest in 1905, but at the moment, it was forcing Swint to take his 5,000 head of cattle about 150 extra miles. Unfortunately, the extra miles translated into ten or more extra days, and much of it without water in order to get around the mountains and to Tucson.

When Bart had ridden for perhaps thirty minutes, he knew he was far enough away that a rifle shot wouldn't scare the cattle. He stopped, took the .45-75 out of the scabbard, levered a shell into the chamber, laid the weapon across the saddle, took aim at a cactus about seventy-five yards away, and squeezed the trigger. When the smoke cleared, Bart saw the bullet had torn a sizeable chunk out of the large plant where he had aimed. The rifle packed a wallop. The good news was the weapon hit where he aimed; the bad news was that firing it was torture on the shoulder. This particular weapon had a twenty-four inch barrel. It wouldn't be very accurate beyond 100 yards. But that was fine for what Bart might need.

This caliber was designed for big game, and it would certainly be a man stopper.

The rifle shot wasn't heard by the cattle, but a small group of Apaches sure heard it. The land was reasonably flat, and the Indians had a fairly good idea where the shot had come from. They kicked their ponies and headed in the direction of the sound. The three Apaches topped a slight rise and saw the white man walking his horse along.

Bart saw the Indians at about the same time they saw him. The Indians were a little more than 200 yards away and charged their horses at Bart.

There was no way he was going to outrun the Apaches, so Bart pulled Buck down and got behind him. When the Indians got to a little less than 100 yards, Bart fired the first time. The impact of the .45-75 slug knocked the Indian off his horse, and when he hit the ground he didn't move. The other two Apaches turned their horses and rode out of sight.

Bart got Buck up and spent the remainder of the day scouting for water and grazing areas and found the latter but not the former. Around dusk, he returned to the camp and reported his observations to Swint. The problem wasn't the lack of water but the inaccessibility of the streams. Bart began to understand the logistical challenges of feeding and watering 5,000 head of cattle over a 300 plus mile trek. To compound the problem, finding the grazing areas and water rested entirely on the shoulders of Homer Barthelme Strong. He was feeling the pressure and the adventure was just starting. Bart had never considered himself a professional scout. He had always left that job to Brubaker and Baxter and their men. His expertise was in finding a Union officer, shooting him, and then finding his way back to the Confederate encampment without being caught. He was plowing new ground with the responsibility Swint had placed on his shoulders. He could read sign, terrain, and choose a route, but the responsibility made him nervous. So much was at stake for Swint based on how well Bart did his job.

The initial problem was finding an adequate place to water the herd and cross the Rio Grande River. It had been raining north of Socorro, which was unusual for the late summer in New Mexico. The rainfall had caused the Rio Puerco, Chama, San Jose, and Salado Rivers to feed more water than usual into the Rio Grande. As a result of the excessive water runoff, the water level in the Rio Grande was higher and swifter than usual. The Rio Grande wasn't out of its banks, but it was right at flood stage and high enough to be threatening to cattle and drovers if they tried to ford the river or water the herd at the wrong place. Where the water depth along a bank had been three feet deep, it was now five to eight feet deep and swift. Dumb cows could slide into the water, be swept away by the current, and drown. Bart realized the initial success of the trail drive depended upon his being able to find a suitable place to water the cattle and cross the Rio Grande.

Cookie brought Bart a cup of hot coffee and a plate of beans he had reheated. He thanked the cook for his kindness and sat against a wagon wheel, ate his food, and drank his coffee. As he was finishing the last of his coffee, Bart looked at Swint and said, "John, I got to meet three Apaches today. I expect one of them is dead."

"Just what we need. I figured the Apaches would steal a cow or two, but I didn't think they would attack us. I guess they figured one old man would be easy pickins."

Bart laughed and replied, "Now that you're a captain, you're a lot nicer than you were when you were a sergeant."

The following morning, Bart was up and gone at daylight. He skipped breakfast and opted for just a cup of coffee instead. This time, he rode Jeff's black stallion and put a small can of Arbuckle, a boiling cup, and a few pieces of jerked meat in his haversack. He headed west until he reached the Rio Grande, then followed the bank of the river south, and looked for a likely spot to take the cattle across. About mid-day, Bart cut the trail of about a half-dozen shod horses heading north by east. It appeared the tracks were about a day old as the horse droppings were dry on the outside. It was possible it could be a small army patrol from Fort Wingate in Seboyeta, New Mexico, but that would have them more than seventy-five miles from their garrison, which didn't make much sense. Of course a five man scouting patrol and a pack horse with supplies was a possibility. Geronimo and his band were still wandering around this part of New Mexico. He had got to meet three of them the day before, but they had unshod horses, unless of course they were riding horses they had stolen from whites. It was also possible it could be outlaws or more likely rustlers who planned to cut Swint's herd. Anything was possible.

Horse tracks will provide a lot of information: whether the rider is large or small, whether or not the horse is shod, and in some cases, will even identify the horse if the tracks have been seen previously. What horse tracks won't do is tell who is riding the horse. Bart built a small fire, boiled a cup of Arbuckle, and picketed the stallion to let him nibble on the grass. While the coffee was boiling, he studied the tracks, but there were too many possibilities to arrive at a useful conclusion.

Late in the afternoon, Bart came upon a likely spot to ford the Rio Grande. The river widened significantly, providing a ford just before a bend which held a deep pool of water. Bart crossed the river to test the worthiness of the location, and the black stallion had no difficulty. Water never reached above the girth strap. The bottom was covered with small rocks and was solid. The water was swift but relatively shallow. All in all, it was about as good a place to water the herd and then cross the river as Bart was likely to find.

When Strong got back to the herd, it was well after dark and supper was long over. He went over to Cookie and asked if he had anything left to make a sandwich. The cook produced some cold biscuits and pulled out a skillet to warm a beef steak he had held back for the old scout. Bart poured himself a cup of coffee, thanked Cookie for his thoughtfulness, and noticed there was another folding camp stool next to Swint's.

John motioned him over and said, "Have a seat. I figured your old butt would appreciate a stool."

"My old butt would appreciate a rocker with a pillow, but thanks."

Strong told Swint about the crossing he had found and recounted the tracks he had cut. Swint said, "I've had a feeling we are being followed. Not near, but I think they are out there, nonetheless. I will put an extra drover on the herd tonight."

After Bart had wolfed down the beef steak, the talk turned to Santa Fe, and Bart told Swint about getting shot and the remarkable woman who nursed him back to health.

Swint looked at Strong and said, "You might should go back to Santa Fe and marry that woman if you survive this trail drive and don't die of old age riding a train back." With that bit of encouragement, Bart got up and turned in for the night.

The next morning, Bart sat down beside John Swint, drank his coffee, and ate a couple flapjacks. When he finished eating he said, "John, can you find the crossing with my directions, or do I need to lead you there by the hand?"

Swint looked offended and said, "Oh, I think I can find it alright without you."

Bart laughed and said, "Well, I just wanted to be sure. I remember Captain Brubaker having to send out a search party once to find your patrol and lead you back to the bivouac area."

Swint bellowed, "That's because General Forrest moved the damn camp, and a heavy fog set in. And you know it!"

Bart laughed and said, "Well, since I found you a crossing, I thought I would ride around a mite and look at the scenery, if it is all right with you."

Swint looked at Bart and responded, "I kinda know what you got up your sleeve. You be careful, bad enough I've got to depend on an ole coot. I don't want you dead. I ain't got time to look for the body and bury you!"

Bart thanked John for his compassion and concern, saddled Buck, looked at Swint, and said, "I might be gone a day or two. Try not to lose sleep worrying about me. And try not to get lost!" He then got tickled by his own humor and had a good laugh before he trotted the buckskin out of the camp heading west. Swint wasn't nearly as amused.

After riding for about ten miles, Bart turned Buck north and rode for a few miles and then turned north by east. This maneuver brought Strong about five miles north of the herd and in rocky foothills. He walked Buck and kept a sharp eye out for movement of any kind in the rocks and small arroyos and valleys below. He just had a hunch!

After a couple miles, Bart saw a flash of light reflect off something and pulled Buck up behind a large boulder and dismounted. The glint of light could be from an empty can or a broken bottle some hunter left, or it could be from a rifle barrel. He took out the Winchester and began slowly making his way through the boulders until he was above the area where he had seen the reflection. He came out from behind a large outcrop of rocks and saw a man about thirty yards from him, sitting against a rock smoking a cigarette and looking at a pocket watch. Now Bart knew what flashed as the sun's rays hit it.

Bart hailed the man and said, "You sit real still. I'm coming down to have a little chat with you." When Bart got to within a few feet of the man, he stopped and asked, "What are you doing out here all by your lonesome?"

"I could ask you the same thing."

"Let me tell you what I think, and then you can chew on it and tell me if I'm wrong. A group of men have been trailing us since we moved our cattle herd from Socorro. Since you are just sitting out here enjoying the sun, it occurs to me you might be waiting to meet someone, perhaps someone from the herd?"

The man blanched and fidgeted a little bit, which was a dead giveaway. Bart went on, "If I were a betting man, I would wager you were here to meet James Smart. He's in a hole in the ground outside Socorro, so he won't be of any help to you. I suggest you tell your friends to give up the idea of cutting this herd and go back wherever you came from." With that, Bart told the man to take his revolver out of the holster really easy like with thumb and forefinger and drop it on the ground. He then told the man to kick the pistol over his way, bent down, picked it up, took out the cylinder, shook the loads into his hand and threw them down the hillside. Then he walked over to the man's horse and pulled his Winchester from its scabbard and ejected the shells.

Bart looked at the man and said, "Remember what I said. If you try to cut our herd it won't go well with you." With that, Strong put the Winchester in the man's scabbard and the pistol in the man's saddle bags, took the lead of the horse, and started walking off.

"You're gonna make me walk back to camp unarmed?"

"Looks like. You have a canteen of water. You will be fine. I will turn your horse loose in a couple miles. You can find him if you like or walk back to your friends." Bart began working himself back to Buck, leading the mustang and rode off to the south towards the herd. After a mile or so, he looped the bridle of the man's horse over the pommel and slapped the mare on the rump. He cut west and went to the crossing area, built a small fire, put on a pot of Arbuckle, loosened the cinch on Buck, and ground picketed him. After the coffee cooked, he drank a cup and then leaned up against a Rio Grande (Fremont) Cottonwood tree, pulled his hat down over his eyes, and took a nap.

When Bart awoke it was late evening. He decided he would just spend the night and wait right there for the herd to arrive. He saw no logic in riding back to the herd just so he could ride back to the crossing again. He took the saddle off Buck, put down his ground cover, filled his pipe, lay back, and examined the stars. The western skies at night were worth all the discomfort of living outside in the elements. He slept well and dreamed of Stella.

Chapter 23

About mid-morning, the first of the herd began arriving at the crossing on the Rio Grande. Bart told Swint about finding the rustler who was waiting for John Smart and sending him back to his friends on foot. John wasn't surprised at all and said he knew they were being followed. Bart told John he was going to be gone a couple days and to move the cattle slowly after they crossed the Rio Grande. John asked Bart what he had up his sleeve, and Strong was evasive, "Just scouting" was his only response.

Strong knew water was going to be scarce if they took the circular route to the south of the mountains because there wasn't much there but sage, rattlesnakes, and alkali pools of water that would kill the cattle. He rode into the Gila Mountains on an old trail and continued on it all day, taking a couple breaks to rest his back and hind end. Late in the afternoon, he stopped at Percha Creek dead tired and made camp. The creek had a decent water flow, and it would be fairly easy to take the cattle across. Early the following morning, Bart set out and rode several miles and then came upon Iron Creek. There was sufficient water running to water the cows, but there was little to no grass to speak of since he had entered the mountains. When he got to the Gila River Valley, there was plenty of grass and, of course, the Gila River, which was more a creek than a river here at its headwaters.

Swint had told Bart that cows could go more than a month without food and up to a week without water. So the mountain crossing could be tolerated by the herd.

Bart saw that there were a couple homesteaders in the valley and rode to the nearest of the two and hailed the cabin. A man and woman and a couple kids came out and waved at Bart. The man said that they rarely saw other humans this far in the wilderness. Bart told the man why he was in the Gila and that he might be leading a few thousand head of longhorn cattle through, and if so, they would bed them in the valley. To help soothe the man's obvious concern, Bart told him they would keep the cattle away from his homestead. The man invited Bart to step down off his horse and have a cup of coffee. Bart thanked the man and declined, saying he needed to get back to the herd. He bid the family good-day, turned Buck around, and started back.

Bart spent the night on the trail and continued to be amazed at how chilly the nights were in the mountains. Even with his ground cover and blanket, he was chilled. He was up and on his way early. When he got back to the herd, he poured himself a cup of coffee and sat on the folding stool next to Swint. John said, "Where have you been and what have you been doing, Bart?"

Bart looked at his old friend and said, "I rode into the Gila and did some looking around. Hear me out before you reject my idea out of hand." Strong then went on to tell Swint about the trail which led through the Gila.

"Bart, you're crazy. You can't drive cattle through the mountains."

"John, the trail is wide enough in most places for three or four cattle to walk side by side. There is nowhere for them to go but down the trail, and there is water in Percha Creek, Iron Creek, and ample pasture in the Gila Valley along with the Gila River. There are a couple homesteaders in the Gila Valley, and I promised them we would keep the cattle away from their places. The weather is much cooler in the mountains, and it should offset some of the energy the cattle will expend making the climb."

John looked at Bart and said, "It's never been done. Nobody has ever tried to take cattle across a mountain."

Strong looked at Swint for a few moments and said, "Well, if you try to go around, you are going to lose several of your cows to thirst. The pilgrims I met in the Gila came around the south side and said there isn't water until you get to the Gila River. And we would be in the open for rustlers or Apaches to cut the herd. They're your cows, so you make the decision."

"I'll think on it but if something went wrong in the mountains and we can't get back out, I could lose the entire herd."

Bart admitted, "There is certainly that possibility because there is no way to turn the herd around before we get to the Gila Valley."

Bart and John sat in silence drinking their coffee for several minutes, and finally, John asked, "Can we get the chuck wagon through on this trail of yours?"

"I've been thinking on that. The trail is wide enough, but it will be snug in places. I would put blinders on the horses and leave three or four drovers with Cookie just in case he gets in trouble." Bart lit his pipe and accepted a plate of beans from Cookie, and the cook refilled his cup. He thanked Cookie for the food and coffee. After allowing the beans to cool and eating the grub, he sipped on the coffee, and relit his pipe.

Finally Swint spoke up and said, "It's a damn fool idea but just crazy enough that it might work."

As they were sitting talking and drinking coffee Strong said to Swint "Has that man on the ridge been dogging you all day? I thought my sending that scout back on foot would have discouraged that bunch."

"Yes, I've seen him on and off most of the day."

Bart got up, walked to the chuck wagon, and asked Cookie to please get his Whitworth out of the wagon. He checked the load and took out a fresh primer and walked over to a wagon wheel.

A young cowboy who was in camp eating said, "What have you got in mind, Mr. Strong?"

"Son, I thought I might wing him a mite to show his friends we aren't pilgrims."

The young man whose name was Joseph Friber responded, "That man is 500 yards away. There is no way you can hit him."

Bart looked at the rider on the ridge for a moment and said, "I'd say closer to 550."

"I'll wager twenty dollars of my drive money you don't hit him."

Swint continued drinking his coffee, never looked up, and said, "Son, you better save your money." Strong rested the Whitworth on the wagon wheel, set the elevation to 600 yards, adjusted the windage just a mite to allow for the slight breeze, engaged the set trigger, took a deep breath, exhaled slowly, and squeezed on the trigger with steady, slightly increasing pressure until the rifle startled him when it discharged. The man grabbed his right shoulder as he fell out of the saddle. Bart looked at him with his binoculars and turned to Swint and said, "I think he will be alright, but I doubt he will be doing any rustling or shooting for a few days."

Young Mister Friber just shook his head and said, "Well, I'll be. If I hadn't seen it with my own eyes, I wouldn't have believed it. Never saw anything like that before."

The next morning, they headed the cattle towards the trail opening in the Gila range. The first part of the trail was a steady incline of about ten degrees for about eight miles, and the cattle labored and started to bunch up before they reached the top. The old brindle steer in the lead just kept plodding along with the herd following him. As the sun got behind the western range and provided some shade, the first of the herd topped the peak and started down the other side. By midafternoon, all five thousand head were on the downward slope. When the majority of the cattle had arrived at the first creek, Bart and the cowboys stopped, built a small fire, and started a pot of coffee. The cattle drank and nibbled on what little grass was available.

Bart had been informed by Swint that driving a herd of cattle was a delicate balance between covering ground and allowing the cattle to rest. Too little rest and the cattle would lose weight, which was money at market. Too much rest and you got to the market late, and you would be sucking hind teat because the market would be glutted with cattle.

There were four drovers with Bart ahead of the herd, and John Swint, three cowboys, the remuda, and the chuck wagon behind the herd. Swint put two drovers in front of the chuck wagon, and he and two drovers rode behind. Bart and the drovers left their saddles on their horses and loosened the cinches to make the mounts more comfortable. If something spooked the herd, they would have to mount quickly and stay ahead of the cattle. There would be no time to saddle a horse. Bart hoped Swint and his crew had a nice meal as he took out a cold biscuit and a piece of jerked meat from his saddle bag. The cattle were tired, thirsty, and restless. But they had nowhere to go so they bedded down and stayed down all night, which was unusual, because cattle normally get up a couple times at night and mill around a little.

At first light, one of the drovers put a little fuel on the hot coals and refilled the coffee pot from a canteen. After Bart and the drovers drank their coffee, they tightened the cinches on their mounts and started up the next incline on the trail. The old brindle bull got up, started walking down the trail, and cattle started following him. A little before sunset, they crested the rise and saw a small valley and Percha Creek about one-half mile away. The cattle rushed to the water and strung out along the bank. As they drank, the drovers would move them across the creek and to the other side to browse on what little foliage there was and make room for more cattle to drink. As the last of the cattle made their way to the creek, the chuck wagon, Swint, the remuda, and the rest of the drovers arrived.

Swint got down from his horse and said, "The cattle are worn out. We will stop here, let them water and eat what little grass there is, rest up tomorrow, and leave the following morning." The cattle were tightly packed in the small valley but seemed content. Cookie got some beef steaks grilling and some biscuits baking in a dutch oven. Bart took the saddle off Buck, rubbed him down with the saddle blanket, then filled his pipe and had a cup of coffee. After about an hour, Bart saddled Blackie and told Swint he was going to ride back a ways and check their back trail. After trotting the horse for almost an hour, stopping at every twist and turn and checking with his binoculars, Bart was confident they weren't being followed. He thought going back and checking was a waste of time. How could rustlers steal a herd they couldn't turn around or get in front of? But one couldn't be too cautious. Bart carefully rode back in the darkness and arrived around 8 PM.

They were about thirty miles into the crossing of the Gila and had about forty-five to go. They spent the next day just lounging around, working on tack, and drinking coffee. They got the cattle started early the following morning and made good time. During late afternoon, they came to Iron Creek and let the cattle drink as they crossed the stream. They bedded the cattle down for the night. They had made about fifteen miles and had about thirty to go to get to the Gila River.

The following day, there were small streams and water runoffs from the snow on the mountain tops but nothing large enough to water 5,000 head of cattle. The drovers kept the cattle moving. Some would take a sip as they crossed the small trickles of water. The cattle really weren't thirsty and were just drinking because the water was there. When they came to a clearing, they stopped for the night and bedded the cattle. They had made about ten miles that day and had about twenty to go.

The next day, the trail began to decline in elevation, and the cattle started a slow trot. A few of the weaker cattle fell off the pace. Cookie stopped the chuck wagon, killed and butchered two cows to feed the drovers, and rolled the rest of their carcasses into the gorge below. They bedded the cattle again and had beef steaks for supper. Just after sunset the following day, they came to the Gila River and a large valley filled with green grass. They had made it! No one had ever attempted to take cattle across a mountain range before, and while it might never be attempted again, it had worked. The timing had been perfect because it was before the weather turned cold; yet it was cool. The water runoff, from the thawing of the remaining snow, which never completely went away, and the spring rains helped fill the Gila River.

John Swint jogged up to Bart and grabbed him in a bear hug, "You did it, you crazy ole coot. You did it, and I figure we lost less than ten head of cattle." Bart reminded Swint that he had promised to keep the cattle away from the farms. John sent three drovers to stay between the herd and the farms and make sure the herd didn't wander in that direction, tear up fences, or destroy gardens.

The remainder of the cattle drive went without incident. Swint got a good price for his beef in Tucson and paid off the drovers. He handed Bart an envelope full of money and said, "Bart, here is your well-deserved share."

Strong looked at Swint and said, "I was just keeping my word to an old friend. We didn't talk about money."

"We didn't talk about money then, and we ain't gonna talk about it now. Take the money and my thanks. Without you, I would have lost a good bit of the herd." They shook hands, and Bart returned the Winchester and cartridges, had Cookie get his Whitworth and scabbard, mounted Buck, and took the lead of his pack horse and the black stallion, and headed for the livery. About half way to the hotel from the livery, Bart was met by Cookie, the trail drive cook. The man said, "Mr. Strong, my name is John Winton, and I appreciate you always asking instead of telling me when you needed something. You are a decent man. Stop by the chuck wagon before you leave. I have something for you." Bart promised John he would stop and see him before he left Tucson.

This was to be the last time Bart and John Swint were to see each other. Two years later, while on a trail drive taking another herd of cattle to market, Swint's horse stepped in a gopher hole while trying to turn some wayward steers, fell, and broke its leg. The freak accident caused Swint to go over the horse's neck, land awkwardly, and break his neck. Swint died the second day after the accident. One of the west's better cattlemen was buried on the trail, which was fitting and what he would have wanted.

Chapter 24

Bart stayed at the Tucson Hotel in Tucson, Arizona, for three days eating some decent food at the Trail's End Café, enjoying decent coffee and a few slices of fairly good apple pie. On the second day, Bart rode out to the trail camp and was greeted by Cookie, aka John Winton, who presented him with a sack. Bart opened the top of the sack and discovered it was full of Bear Sign. He could have kissed the man. There was nothing better than, or rarer than, donuts on the frontier. The fact the camp cook cared enough to make Bart a batch of Bear Sign was an honor. Bart thanked John for the gift and wished him well.

Bart knew he had a decision to make and wasn't enjoying the inner turmoil associated with his assessment. He realized he wasn't getting any younger. It was September 14, 1880, and Bart had just celebrated his sixty-fifth birthday on August 3. Life came with no guarantees. He could spend years looking for Buryl Weathers, the last man on his execution list, with no guarantee he would ever find him. Also, the way he was aging, there was no guarantee his health would allow him to continue his quest. He was tired, bone tired, after looking for killers for almost eighteen months. Tracking after men was a physically and emotionally taxing experience. The nights sleeping, or trying to sleep on the hard ground took its toll over time. Always wondering if a killer was waiting for him around the next bend in the trail or boulder kept your nerves on edge. Killing other human beings, no matter how vile they were, took its toll. Bart realized the hardships of trail life were degrading his mind, body, energy, and resolve. The years he might trail after Weathers, with or without success could maybe be spent in Santa Fe with Stella, if she would have him. The option between chasing a man he might never catch and catching a woman he loved was getting easier the more he considered the choice.

Bart made his decision, the only decision that made any sense. He went to the livery, haggled with the hostler, and sold the pack horse for less than he was worth. He then went to the railroad station and bought a coach ticket for himself and two livestock tickets for Buck and Blackie on the Southern Pacific railroad all the way through to Albuquerque, New Mexico. Once the horses were in the livestock car, Bart wrapped their legs and placed shipping blankets he had purchased on them. Bart placed his saddle and panniers with the horses and stayed with, and kept them soothed. He made sure their tethers were long enough to allow them to keep their balance. Bart spent part of his time in the coach car and would periodically go to the livestock car and make sure both horses were calm and being cared for. He took it upon himself to clean the stalls and make sure they were watered and calmed them as best he could.

When they arrived in Albuquerque for a layover, Bart personally took the horses, his saddle, Whitworth, Greener, panniers, and haversack off the train and led the mounts to the livery. After he was sure the hostler would attend to Buck and Blackie, Bart went to the Corn Exchange Hotel and checked in for the night.

The following morning, Bart went to the La Placita Dining Room for breakfast and then went to the train depot to make arrangements to load the two horses for the short trip to Santa Fe, only to discover the locomotive had some kind of mechanical problem and would be a day replacing a broken part. Bart had checked out of the Corn Exchange Hotel, so he went down the street to the St. James Hotel and checked in there. He went back to the La Placita for dinner, checked on the horses, and retired for the evening.

The next morning, it was back to the La Placita and then to the depot where he found the train would be leaving right after lunch. Bart went to the livery and retrieved Buck and Blackie, and took them to the livestock car and got them settled in. He had sat the saddle on Buck and the panniers on Blackie and carried his Whitworth, Greener, and haversack. He placed the saddle and panniers on the floor next to the horses. Since it wasn't that far from Albuquerque to Santa Fe, Bart just bought himself the cheapest coach ticket and spent most of the trip with the horses.

On the short run to Santa Fe, a gang of outlaws boarded the train on an incline which slowed the train enough to allow them to ride their horses alongside and jump aboard. Bart was in the livestock car with Buck and Blackie when he saw a horse with an empty saddle running alongside the train. Bart made sure the Greener was loaded, left the livestock car, looked into the first coach car, and saw a familiar face from the past. It was Jesse Woodson James, a man he remembered vividly from his time with Quantrill's Raiders and Bloody Bill Anderson's bushwhackers, not out of fondness either.

Bart had read about the James gang bungling a bank robbery in Northfield,

Minnesota, and losing all the gang members to death or prison. Jesse James and his brother Frank had managed to escape the posse and made it back to Missouri. Obviously, James had picked up some recruits and had traveled far from Missouri to rob this train. When Bart entered the coach, James had gone into the next coach. Strong had his Greener at the ready and walked down the aisle as a bandit was preoccupied with taking money and possessions from passengers. When Strong got to within about ten feet, he hollered for the man to throw down his pistol. Instead, the man turned and was trying to bring his pistol to bear on Bart and was met with a load of buckshot. The load of buckshot knocked the man off his feet and against the coach door. Bart got a passenger to help him drag the body out of the way. Bart took out the spent shell, replaced it with another load of buckshot, and open the coach door.

Strong stood on the landing between the two cars, peeked through the small window in the door, and saw Jesse James. He opened the second coach door and stepped inside with the shotgun pointed at James. Bart then hollered to James to give it up and get off the train. Men in the first coach had gotten out their firearms, and were starting to come into the coach behind him. Bart told them to stay calm. The last thing he needed was a hail of bullets which would just as likely kill him as the outlaws.

James could see the handwriting on the wall that he was severely outgunned and outmaneuvered. His thoughts turned to the fiasco in Northfield.

James hollered, "Who the heck are you, ole man?"

Bart hollered back, "Bart Strong, you little squirt. You were a back shooting piss ant during the war and haven't changed. Get the heck off this train and go back to Missouri and steal chickens while you are still sucking air."

James and his remaining gang members jumped off the train, rounded up their horses, and headed back to Missouri. What was left of the James gang robbed two stores in western Mississippi and a bank in southern Tennessee after the botched attempt to rob the train with Strong aboard. The glory days of the James gang robbing banks and trains were over. The gang, such as it was, resorted to petty theft, robbing dry goods stores and stage coach relay stations just to feed themselves and their mounts. Jesse James was killed on April 3, 1882, in Saint Joseph, Missouri, by one of his cousins.

Bart finally arrived in Santa Fe in the late afternoon on September 18, 1880, tired and out of sorts. After taking his horses to the livery, he went to the bathhouse, bought a tub of hot water, and soaked while his clothes were being cleaned. He went to the barber shop, got a shave and hair trim, and started feeling a little more civilized. When he came out of the barber shop, people were gathered around and asking him questions about the foiled robbery and if it was really Jesse James who tried to rob the train. Bart just smiled slightly and told the small crowd to talk to the passengers. He then headed for Stella Goodson's boarding house. He was worried about how he would be received by Stella and what future, if any; he was to have with her.

When Bart started up the stairs to the porch, Stella came running out and fairly well leaped into his arms almost knocking him to the ground. In fact, he had to drop the Whitfield and Greener in order to catch her. The first words out of her mouth were, "Yes, I will marry you, and at your age, I don't think we should have a long engagement. Do you have any plans for the Saturday after next?" Bart really didn't know what to say. It was like a tornado had engulfed him. He kinda grinned and said, "I guess I do now."

"Maybe if you have a wife and responsibilities, you won't go traipsing off chasing outlaws."

Homer Barthelme Strong and Stella Mae Goodson were married in the oldest church in the United States, San Miguel Chapel, in Santa Fe, New Mexico. Half the residents of Santa Fe showed up for the wedding. Most of the people of Santa Fe didn't know Bart from Adam's house cat, but everyone in the town knew and liked Stella. The reception after the wedding lasted well into the night with Mexican music and enough food for an army. Stella had told her boarders she was going to be out of town for a few days, and they would have to get their meals at the Miss Woody Café until she returned.

Having had enough of trains, Bart rented a buggy and a stable horse. They loaded their grips in the back and left for Albuquerque, New Mexico, and were greeted with whistles and shouts as they drove off. Once outside Santa Fe, Bart stopped and untied the old pots, cans, and other things from the rig. They spent two evenings on the road in waystations and stayed three nights in the big city. They saw one play and went to a music theatre. They enjoyed some of the finer restaurants and took in all the sites. They returned home, staying at the same places on the return trip.

When Bart and Stella returned to the boarding house he found a note from Ned

Buntline, aka Edward Judson, a writer of dime novels about the west. He was staying at the La Fonda Hotel and wanted to see Bart as soon as he arrived. Buntline had gotten wind of Strong's quest to find the killers of his family and wanted to interview him to get some details for a new book. Bart had no interest in helping the writer fabricate a story but knew he would hound him until he agreed to meet. After the Strongs got unpacked and Stella checked in with the boarders, Bart walked to the La Fonda.

Bart sat down with Buntline and told him straight off he had no interest in sharing any of the details regarding his tracking of his family's killers and bringing them to justice. He told Buntline he had read about him taking great liberties with facts and details and having even made up stories about himself. Buntline didn't appear to be offended by Bart's comment and told him he would make him famous. Bart looked at Buntline and replied, "I don't want to be famous. I just want to be left alone to live the rest of my life in obscurity." With that he got up and walked back to the boarding house.

The livery charged a modest rate for caring for Buck and Blackie, so Bart decided to leave them in the care of the hostler rather than building a stable. Bart spent some time in the telegraph office arranging to have his funds transferred from Bolivar, Missouri, to the First National Bank of Santa Fe, New Mexico, which just happened to be the oldest bank in the southwestern United States. He then sent a telegram to a friend in Bolivar, Missouri, to start the process of selling his home there. Every couple of weeks, Bart would take out his weapons and clean them. In the back of his mind was the possibility the hunter could again become the hunted. Buryl Weathers would have no way of knowing he had given up the chase and might possibly come looking for him. Bart stored the Whitworth but kept the Greener loaded and within quick reach in the house. He decided it would be prudent to carry the pistol wherever he went. If Weathers got close and gave him enough notice, he might be able to hit him with a shot from the S & W revolver. At any rate, having the pistol on his side made him feel more secure.

Having taken care of his business, or as much as he could until the house in Missouri sold, Bart turned his attention to doing a little landscaping behind the boarding house. Bart and Stella had been married for two months. They were very compatible and enjoyed each other's company immensely, but Bart was bored out of his mind. He had always been busy, and now he had nothing to occupy his time other than pulling weeds and stacking rocks. He had nothing to give him a reason to get out of bed in the morning, no challenges.

Bart had no interest in practicing law. He didn't want to defend the guilty. And writing wills and real estate contracts just wouldn't be his cup of tea. He was too old to be a lawman, and Santa Fe had a fine city marshal and the county a fine sheriff anyway. Sometimes life has a way of working itself out, and in Bart's case, it did.

Chapter 25

November 3, 1880 started off much like most mornings since Bart and Stella had married. Bart finished his second cup of coffee and walked to the livery to check on Buck and Blackie rub their heads a mite and say hello. After spending a few minutes with the horses, Bart walked back home with the intent of doing some minor repairs on the house.

When he walked into the house he didn't see Stella, so he went into the kitchen to give her a hug before starting work. When he walked in, he saw her sitting at the kitchen table. She didn't move and Bart said, "Stella, are you alright?"

"I dunt ko, I feel frunny."

Bart walked around in front of Stella and saw that her face was distorted on one side and her mouth was drooped open on the same side. He had no idea what was going on, but he knew it wasn't good. He picked Stella up, carried her to the sofa in the foyer, put her down, and ran out of the house and to the doctor's office.

Doc Spencer was in his office when Bart came bursting in and said, "What's wrong Bart?"

"It's Stella, I don't know what's wrong, but she is confused and having trouble talking."

Doc Spencer grabbed his medical bag and he and Bart scurried down the street to the boarding house as quickly as they could.

Doc Spencer stooped by the sofa and examined Stella. In a few minutes he turned to Bart and said, "Stella has suffered what we call a stroke. It's when a blood vessel in the brain is blocked. I've read some medical information on a treatment which involves salicylic acid. I have a small amount in my office that a medicine drummer left for me to try under the right circumstances. I think we should try it with Stella and see if it helps."

"How serious is this, Doc?"

"Bart, I don't want to unduly worry you, but most people who suffer a stroke never recover and most die within a day or so."

"But she seemed so healthy, how could this happen."

"It's caused by a blockage and there's no known way to prevent it from happening."

Doc Spencer left, went to his office, got the salicylic acid, returned, and gave a spoon full to Stella. She made a face and said, "Dat hurrible."

Doc Spencer smiled and said, "It's just going to be a waiting game, Bart. There is nothing else I can do."

After the doctor left, Bart picked Stella up, carried her to their bedroom, and laid her on the bed.

A hundred things were going through Bart's mind as he tried to make some sense of what was happening. When Mary had died, Bart felt as if his entire world had ended. In some ways this was worse. Stella was there in front of him, but she didn't seem to know what was going on around her.

When the boarders started coming in, Bart told them that Stella had some type of attack and they would have to get their meals elsewhere until he could get some help for the boarding house. They all expressed their regrets and said they understood.

Bart sat by Stella's side all afternoon and all through the night without sleep. Around 7 AM Stella squeezed Bart's arm and said, "Hi honey." She had a slight slur to her words but at least she seemed aware of her surroundings and knew what was going on.

Bart helped Stella get into her night clothes and robe and walked with her to the foyer. He helped her get seated in a comfortable chair and handed her an old newspaper to read as he went to get her some coffee going and fix her a bite to eat.

When he came back, Stella was sitting in the chair crying.

"What's wrong Stella?"

"Bart, I can't read a word on this newspaper. Not a word."

Stella seemed fine in a week or so, but she couldn't read. In fact, she didn't even know what the letters meant.

Slowly but surely, Stella improved. Bart went to the mercantile store and purchased a McGuffey's Eclectic Primer and began teaching Stella the ABCs as if she was a young child. By Christmas, Stella had made great progress and was able to read the primer. It was going to be a long recovery, but she was well on her way.

Chapter 26

On a cold and windy Monday morning on January 3, 1881, the county commissioners for Santa Fe County came to the Goodson/Strong boarding house and asked to speak to Judge Strong. Bart came into the parlor, greeted the men, and shook hands with each. Strong had met them all before at church and social functions, so there was no need for introductions. The gist of the visit was simple. Judge Howard Jackson had suffered a massive heart attack and died. His death left his position on the bench vacant for almost four years as his fourth term had just started. The men wanted to know if Strong would consider filling the vacant seat until the next general election and a new judge could be elected. The spokesman for the group went on to say that the territorial governor had been contacted and would be happy to appoint Judge Strong to fill the vacancy. Bart's first impulse was to kiss each of them, on the lips, but he tried to remain dignified and said, "I would be honored to fill the vacant seat until the election."

Lewis Wallace, the territorial governor, was contacted and informed that Judge Strong would be willing to fill the remainder of Judge Jackson's term. When court went in session the following Monday,

January 10th, Judge Strong was a member of the New Mexico territorial bar and presiding circuit judge for Santa Fe, New Mexico. Thus began Judge Strong's second judgeship which was to last until January 1889. Wallace and Strong hadn't been friends during the Civil War. In fact, they fought on different sides, but they had met several times after the war. And each held the other in high esteem. Governor Wallace is perhaps best known for his novel, *Ben Hur: A Tale of the Christ*, which was published in 1880.

Stella didn't want people to know that she was struggling with reading, so Bart would write down the lists for the mercantile store. The court was recessed at 12 PM every day, Monday through Friday until 2 PM while Bart ate lunch and helped Stella with her reading lessons. By Christmas, 1881, Stella was pretty much back to her old self and was reading better than most people of the period. Her recovery had amazed and pleased Doc Spencer. Bart wasn't amazed in the least, he knew Stella was made of tough material, but he was pleased to see her well again.

In early December 1882, just a couple days before the Christmas break, Judge Strong was in his chambers, having a second cup of morning coffee, and checking his docket for the day when he saw the name Ike

Truebud. Bart rubbed his chin and wondered to himself why that name struck a chord with him.

When the clerk called the case, which was an arraignment hearing, in walked Ira Truebud, shackled and as big as life and just as nasty looking as the first time they had met. There were three cowboys also wearing wrist irons that looked like the three that had been with Truebud when they were chasing the supposed horse thief. The clerk read the charges, and Judge Strong looked at Robert Frederickson, the Prosecuting Attorney for Santa Fe County, and said, "Mr. Fredrickson, let's hear what you've got."

Prosecutor Fredrickson stood and said, "Your honor, Mr. Truebud here was caught in the act of beating a young drover, one Michael Bivens of Utah, with a branding iron."

Judge Strong looked at Ira Truebud for a few moments and said, "Well, if nothing else you are a man of your word. You said you would see me again. Are you represented by counsel?"

Truebud looked at Judge Strong and said, "I don't need a damn lawyer."

Judge Strong looked at Truebud and responded, "That 'damn' will cost you $50.00. I suggest you show respect for this court, or your problems will increase."

Judge Strong looked at the prosecutor and asked, "Who caught him, Mr. Fredrickson?"

"Sheriff Johnson" was the response. Judge Strong asked Sheriff Johnson to take the witness chair and had the bailiff swear him in. Judge Strong looked at Fredrickson and said, "OK, Bob, go ahead with your questions."

Mr. Fredrickson asked Sheriff Johnson to explain what he had seen. The sheriff explained that he was returning from delivering a prisoner to Albuquerque and was on his way back to Santa Fe. When he rode up on a small ridge, he saw Mr. Truebud beating a man with a branding iron. The young man Mr. Truebud was beating was bleeding and appeared unconscious. The sheriff then proceeded to arrest Mr. Truebud and the three drovers. Sheriff Johnson explained that he had two of the cowboys keep the injured man in the saddle while they rode slowly to Santa Fe so he could receive medical treatment. There was a few hundred cows that were left grazing when he brought Truebud and the drovers in. Sheriff Johnson said he later discovered the man's name was Michael Bivens of Moab, Utah.

Judge Strong looked at Ira Truebud and asked, "Do you have any questions for

Sheriff Johnson?" Truebud just shook his head from side to side.

Judge Strong thanked Sheriff Johnson and said he was dismissed. Judge Strong looked at Mr. Fredrickson and asked him where Mr. Bivens was currently located.

Mr. Fredrickson stood and said that Doctor Everett Burke, the new sawbones from Saint Louis, Missouri, had him in a bed behind his office and was trying to keep the boy alive, but it was touch and go as to whether he would succeed. The boy had been badly beaten.

Judge Strong looked at Ira Truebud with scorn and said, "Mr. Truebud, how do you plead?"

Truebud looked at the judge and said, "The man stole one of my horses, and I was teaching him not to steal from me. I could have hung him. We were on our way back to Texas with a couple hundred cows we hadn't sold after delivering a herd of cattle for reservation beef. The man stole one of my horses while we were asleep."

Judge Strong looked at Mister Truebud and said, "Perhaps you didn't understand the question. How do you plead: guilty or not guilty?"

Truebud started in again about the horses and his right to hang the man, and then Judge Strong cut him off and said, "Mr.

Truebud, this is an arraignment hearing, not a trial. All I want to hear from you is how you plead: guilty or not guilty?"

Judge Strong went on to explain to those in attendance that it was customary for a traveling man whose horse broke down to rope another horse and leave his. The theory being that it might be the owner of the horse which was taken in the exchange who might need a remount the next time. Judge Strong went on to say that Mister Truebud had lived in the west for years and without a doubt knew the custom. Judge Strong looked at Truebud and said, "Mister Truebud, did the man leave you his horse when he took your animal?"

Truebud said, "How the hell would I know?"

Judge Strong hit his gavel and said, "That 'hell' will cost you $100.00, the next off color remark will be $200.00. Now, I will ask you again: did Mister Bivens leave you his horse?"

Truebud was mad and red in the face but only admitted that he didn't know if the man left a horse or not, but he was riding a Truebud branded horse when he was caught leaving their camp.

Judge Strong looked at the three drovers and asked the bailiff to swear them in. He then asked each of them if Mister

Bivens had told Truebud that he had left his horse, and each man answered in the affirmative. Judge Strong looked at Sheriff Johnson and asked him if he had seen any of the three drover's strike Mister Bivens. The sheriff said, "No, your honor, the only man I saw beating Mister Bivens was that man, Mister Truebud." Judge Strong told the sheriff to take the wrist cuffs off the drovers and release them. He then told the ranch hands to stay in the area until the trial.

Judge Strong looked at Truebud and said, "You think you cut a mighty wide swathe out here threatening and beating people you have outnumbered. I am entering a plea of not guilty and binding you over for trial for malicious intent, assault and battery, and the attempted murder of Michael Bivens. If he dies, you will be charged with murder and may swing from one of those trees you are so anxious to use on horse thieves and cattle rustlers. This isn't Texas, Mister Truebud."

Bivens lived, and at the trial Ira Truebud was found guilty of attempted murder. Judge Strong ordered Truebud to pay Bivens' medical expenses and awarded the man $1,000.00 in compensation for pain and suffering and the time lost in his travels. In consideration of Ira Truebud's age, Judge Strong sentenced him to only two years in the

Texas State penitentiary at Huntsville, Texas, and to pay $1,000.00 in court costs.

Judge Strong looked at the three drovers and said, "You men are free to go. I suppose your employer just went to prison. I hope you find work on a better ranch."

In the second year of Judge Strong's tenure Deputy U. S. Marshal Frank McGuire knocked on the door of his chambers and stuck his head in, "Can I speak to you for a minute, your honor?"

Strong looked at him and said, "Frank, you know you don't need an appointment here. Come on in." Judge Strong pulled out his pipe and McGuire fired up a cheroot. Judge Strong said, "What's on your mind, Frank."

"Well, your honor, I have some news I thought might be of interest to you. Deputy U.S. Marshall Bob McDougal out of Amarillo, Texas, just picked up a prisoner on a Texas warrant. He told me a group of bandits tried to rob the Missouri-Kansas-Texas Railroad about two weeks ago and encountered a bit of bad luck. Seems the train was carrying five Texas Rangers who were being transported from El Paso to their new post in Fort Worth, Texas. When the bandits burst into the passenger car, the rangers cut loose with their pistols and shotguns and killed two of the three robbers and wounded another and the rest got away."

Judge Strong looked at McGuire quizzically and said, "Well, Frank, that's an interesting story, and they certainly got what they deserved. But why would it be of particular interest to me?"

Frank smiled a wry smile and said, "The one bandit who lived identified the two deceased bandits. One was a fellow named Buryl Weathers. I just thought you might like to know." Frank went on to say that the man said Weathers constantly talked about killing a Judge Strong, the man who shot him in the upper leg and caused him to lose his left eye. It seemed Weathers stopped on the trail to smoke a cigarette and was leaning against a large rock when Judge Strong took a shot at him, and rock shards from the round went into his eye socket. I told McDougal that claim was complete balderdash. If the Bart Strong I knew had a clear shot at Weathers, he would have been dead, not robbing trains. Judge Strong just smiled and made no comment.

Bart looked away, and his eyes started to tear up. The news closed a chapter in his life, but it also left a void that had been filled with hatred. He thanked Frank for coming by and bringing the news and pulled a leather binder out of his desk and put the current date and the name Buryl Weathers on a form and signed it. There were none left.

A sad and sordid chapter of his life was finally over. Nothing could bring back his daughter and he had been robbed of his grandchildren without having ever seen them. But the hating was over at last. The sadness would always be there, but the bitterness could now slowly diminish.

Shortly after Marshall McGuire left, the bailiff knocked on his door and said, "Your honor, there are two rather rough looking cowboys here who say they know you and would like a word."

"Must be the day for visitors. Send them in." When the door opened, two tall thin men with huge moustaches entered. The taller of the two said, "Hello, Corporal Strong." Strong stood and exclaimed, "My God! Lieutenant Baxter and Captain Brubaker, it has been almost twenty years."

Bill smiled and said, "Judge Strong, it's Bill and Bud now, and seventeen years have come and gone since we all mustered out at Corinth, Mississippi." Bud laughed and said, "My question is how in the heck did you find your way back to Missouri without us scouting a path for you?" Bud roared in laughter at his joke, and Bill and Bart just grinned. During the Civil War, Captain Bill Brubaker was the chief of scouts for General

Nathan Bedford Forrest, and he and Bud helped Strong plan safe routes to return to their encampment after sniper missions.

Bill and Bud were on their way back to their ranch after the funeral of Bud's father in the Huzzah valley in Crawford County, Missouri. They had caught a train to Santa Fe to explore the possibility of purchasing some mixed breed cattle. While eating in the Missy Woods Café, they overheard two men talking about a judge who had tracked down and killed the men who murdered his family. They wanted to know if the Strong who pursued the killers was the Bart Strong they had known during the war.

"I am the Strong who tracked them down, but I think it was more luck than skill. You fellows have to come to dinner. Stella would love to meet you after hearing me talk of the two of you so often."

Bill and Bud stayed overnight in the Goodson/Strong boarding house, visiting long into the night reminiscing, telling jokes, ribbing each other, and consuming a bottle of Bart's best bourbon. It was a wonderful, heartwarming visit for all three men. The following morning after breakfast, and goodbyes, Bill and Bud left to return to Montana.

Judge Strong offered himself as a candidate in the general election in

November of 1884 and won with a little more than 75% of the vote. Judge Strong didn't run for reelection in 1888 and retired in January 1889 when the newly elected judge was seated. Judge Strong was considered to have been a fair and impartial arbiter of the law and treated every defendant and claimant whether Mexican, Anglo, or Negro the same regardless of their status or wealth.

Following his retirement from the bench, he and Stella talked about taking a steamship trip up the coast of the great northwest and then on to see Alaska. They laid plans for the trip several times, but something always came up which prevented them from going. The years rolled by, and Bart and Stella enjoyed long walks together and took buggy rides to the Santa Fe River and had their picnics.

Bart had a massive stroke on May 3, 1896 and died two days later at almost eighty years of age. Stella had him laid to rest in the cemetery at the San Miguel Chapel where they had been married. He had a simple tombstone which merely displayed:

Homer Barthelme (Bart) Strong
8-3-1816 — 5-5-1896
Loving husband and father

The Santa Fe Mexican newspaper estimated the mourners in the chapel and those who stood outside at more than 1,000. More than 100 Western Union messages of condolence were received by Stella Strong. Governor Miguel A. Otero and several other government officials attended the funeral. Miguel Otero was to write several western novels, including *The Real Billy the Kid*, published in 1936.

Strong was the quintessential western man, modest but unwavering and uncompromising in his commitment to the law and justice. The story of his quest for retribution for the murder of his family was the thing of which western folklore is made. Several western novels would incorporate elements of his pursuit of the murderers into their storylines.

Stella never remarried and discouraged any would be suitor out of hand. She continued to run the boarding house until she died on June 3, 1921 at ninety-three years of age and was buried beside Bart. Stella left the Goodson-Strong boarding house to the Santa Fe historical society.

The Cattlemen

Chapter 1

James Budwell (Bud) Baxter was a long drink of water, about 6' 4" tall and extremely thin. Bud was the type person who would have to stand in the same place twice just to cast a shadow. He had rusty red hair, a large mustache, and a scar above his left eye from a musket ball which grazed him in a hunting accident. Bud was gregarious and met mighty few strangers. Having a conversation with Bud wasn't much of a problem because he would do most of the talking.

William Travis (Bill) Brubaker was Bud's polar opposite in many ways. Bill was also tall, 6'0' in his stocking feet, but there the comparison ended. He had dark brown hair and wore it shoulder length and kept a well-trimmed Van Dyke beard. Bill was quiet and introspective and rarely commented on anything without giving it due consideration and factoring in the implications. As much as Bud was willing to talk, Bill was more inclined to listen and liked to say, "You can't get in much trouble listening."

Bud and Bill were both born on the same day in 1840, Bud was born at 10:00 PM, and Bill shortly before 11:00 PM on July 7. Both men would joke they had never been more than one hour apart their entire life. Both men were born and grew up on farms in Crawford County, Missouri, in an area now known as the Huzzah Valley. Both the Baxter and Brubaker families owned fairly large farms near the confluence of the Courtois and Meramec Rivers. The bottom land soil was rich and afforded excellent permanent pasture for grazing cattle.

Bud and Bill wanted to be cowboys. They had read the Saint Louis Dispatch which carried stories about Indians and cattle drives in Texas. They devoured penny novels about the west, gunslingers, cattlemen, and Indians and wanted to be a part of the lifestyle. Both young men thought they knew cattle because both farms raised mixed breed Hereford beef cattle. The purebred Hereford originated in Herefordshire in the West Midlands of England and was first brought to America in 1817 when Henry Clay brought a cow, a heifer, and a young bull to his Kentucky farm. The Baxter and Brubaker cattle were distant descendants of those cattle. Once Bud and Bill made it to the west and had to deal with Texas Longhorn cattle, they were to realize they didn't know beans about cows.

239

****

The elder Baxter and Brubaker knew their sons were going to be headed out for the west and adventure sooner rather than later. On their birthday in 1858, both fathers gave their sons Colt Paterson .36 caliber revolvers and ten inch Bowie knives the local blacksmith, who was accomplished at making blades, made for them. Both young men knew they would need a rifle to hunt game and protect themselves at greater distances than a pistol could provide. Both men worked part-time on other farms and saved every penny they were paid. In 1857, both young men had taken part of their savings and rode the forty mile trip to Pacific, Missouri, to Bradford's Gun Shop and purchased two of the second model 1851 Sharps rifle. The rifle shot the .52 caliber cartridge and fired a 475 grain projectile. The Sharps rifle they purchased was manufactured by the Robbins & Lawrence Company of Windsor, Vermont, which developed the weapon for mass production.

In August of 1858, Bud and Bill were at the Meramec Saloon and Eatery in Steeleville, Missouri, when one of the Nuence men made a loud and disparaging remark about Bill's younger sister Mae. Bill turned and looked at the man and said "Fid Nuence, you need to take that lie back."

Nuence looked at him and said, "Or what, Sonny?"

The Cattlemen will be available during the spring of 2019.

Bill Shuey is the author of several books and the weekly ObverseView column. He travels extensively in his Recreational Vehicle with his wife Gloria and his fly rods.

He can be contacted at:
billshueybooks@gmail.com or at his website: www.billshueybooks.com

Made in the USA
Columbia, SC
21 July 2021